TALES OF
ELHAANAI

Cover design by Karl Thomas

Printed in the United States of America
First Printing, 2020
ISBN 978-1-7349192-1-9
Library of Congress Control Number: 2020906693

Dedication

There are so many people who helped me bring this book to life. But the most important is my Lord, who gave me all the inspiration and determination to not only start, but finish. I want to thank my mother who taught me by example in writing and publishing her own book in 2019. I thank my father who is the master of patience and loves reading just as much as I do. My husband, who is great at 'big picture' thinking, complementing my 'it's about the details' tendencies. My daughter, who is very excited that mommy wrote a book. To my Aunt Vi, who helped edit this book and provided wonderful feedback. To Laura Thompson, a God-sent second pair of eyes. To all the church aunties, uncles, cousins and sister-friends who encouraged me to do this, THANK YOU! THANK YOU! THANK YOU!

To all who purchased or borrowed this to read THANK YOU too. My favorite scripture is Romans 5:1-5, our struggles can create in us character and hope if we follow The One. We all have struggles in varying degrees, only you can choose how those struggles will shape you.

Be blessed.

INDEX

Chapter 1

WE WERE SUPPOSED TO DIE together, my love and I. But here I lay among the winter leaves and skeletal branches, alone, but not quite. I can still sense his heartbeat within me. The child lives; but not for long. I didn't have the strength to erect a shield fast enough, and one arrow met its mark. He'd shot me in the back. The coward! Even now, I can feel the point of it grazing the inside of my large belly as I drift off… into the past.

6 months earlier...

"Coming for breakfast my love? My son needs to grow strong; and you are wasting away before my very eyes!"

It seems like only yesterday that we'd been married, not twenty wonderful, though childless, years. What I carry now is a miracle, and I made a promise to The One that I would not speak until his birth.

Regardless, my husband and I are true soul mates, so telepathy is one of our gifts.

"No husband, I have developed an aversion to the scent of the dining hall of late. I'll have the cook bring me porridge or soup. But you go and enjoy. Give my wishes to your sister and nephew."

"As you wish Dear. I will return shortly, and we can take a walk through your garden. The season is changing and the leaves have turned the most wonderful shades of bronze and gold. The fresh air will do you both much good. And if you get too tired, I can still carry you… like I did so many years ago over this very threshold."

He cups my face, and I lean into him. *"Alanna, my love for you grows tenfold each day."*

"And I you, my King. I will look forward to it."

Only, he never returns. I feel the moment our bond shatters as though my very soul has been ripped from me. The last thoughts I receive from him are, "*We are betrayed! Devona! Run Alanna, run!*" And run I do.

From the moment the Oracle had predicted that a son would be born to us, my sister-in-law Devona had grown cold towards me. When her son, David, had been heir to the throne, we had been the best of friends. Alas, no longer. In secret, I had a small pack prepared for both my husband and I, should the need ever arise.

Sadly, as fate would have it, I alone have need of it now. I linger only long enough to cast a spell of my likeness reclining in the bed, before slipping through the secret door in our chambers.

This is not the walk through the gardens my husband promised, nevertheless, it is a walk I must take. Shrouded in the Oracle's enchanted cloak, my footsteps can neither be heard nor followed. As I race through the gardens, soldiers repeatedly cross my path, swords drawn, sometimes barely an arm's reach away. The forest loomed ahead, casting one final gaze behind me to my home, Nuru Manor, named for the light we believed in. The encroaching fog blotting out the light just as Devona's darkness sought to blot out the light I carried with me. Stepping off our lands I knew only another enchantress would be able to locate me, and with much effort. For I, Alanna Bear-Claw, am Queen *and* High Priestess of Elhaanai. Not many are born with gifts, and even fewer are knowledgeable enough to be able to wield them. Although my parents' gifts had been weak, somehow I had been born with an abundance of them. One special gift had been revealed to me, the knowledge that this child would be gifted as well. I had foreseen great strength, as had the Oracle.

The last time we spoke her words had been a warning. "Mistress, this child will possess power like none have seen since the days of Elrond! You must have a care. There are those who will seek to destroy him, before and after his birth. I have prepared this cloak for you should you have need. It will hide your existence, as long as I live."

I had bowed my head in acknowledgment. Though my heart had pounded with fear, I had accepted the garment and hid it in our chamber. That night, the internal conversation between my love and I had been quite strained.

"Kaison, what the Oracle told me is true! I can feel it. We must consider the threats."

"Rest easy. No one would dare harm either of you while I live. I will assign another guard or ten to dispense this fear if you wish. What about Akronius? He is the most skilled man we have."

"No, be serious, his loyalty lies with your sister and his propensity for violence is unsettling. You are not even listening. What of Devona? Are you not concerned she will try to keep her son as heir? This child is a direct threat to hers. You know she has always coveted the crown."

"Devona wouldn't dare."

"I believe she would. You are aware she has started dabbling with the dark arts."

"Only as a hobby, she has no natural born gifting, and seeks only to..."

"To usurp your throne through her son and align herself with our enemies!"

"Calm down my love, I hear you, and will look into it. Do not stress yourself or the child. I will handle it."

"See that you do. Now, come rub my belly. You have upset your child, and he is kicking me in protest!"

"Ahh! Now that is something I can do, my cherished one. Hello little one... little Alric."

Chapter 2

IT SEEMS SO LONG AGO, but it has only been a few weeks. At nine months, the child is due any day now and still I am being pursued. There are spies everywhere. The moment I let my hood down, I can feel their eyes on me. The baying of the hounds tracking me day after day, night after night sends chills racing down my arms. Cuts and bruises mar my arms and legs, but I do not cry. I have neither the time nor energy to dedicate toward tears. Everything I have is used just to take the next step.

Yesterday I reached the river's edge, but it had taken me too long. The trackers are on my heels. The river is raging with runoff from the mountains, so I cannot safely cross it. If I was strong enough and had time, I could use my gifts to pass. The river before me, the hounds behind, and I feel my final protection fading. The shroud begins to change around me. Devona must have finally killed the Oracle. I turn to face my murderers. As I wait, I let my power flow through to my fingertips, praying to The One, that I have enough left.

No words are spoken as they form a semicircle around me, crossbows are raised and arrows loosed. Air leaves me in a rush with the impact of an arrow hitting my leg; a second pierces my back and brings me to my knees.

As I lie bleeding, one brave, or very stupid, attacker has sauntered over to whisper in my ear.

"How low the mighty have fallen! Your brat will never be born, never know who his father was and never know you. My queen and her son will finally reign as they were meant to, and we will rule this land with an iron fist! Take solace in knowing we didn't make you suffer like the Oracle, well, you won't suffer *as* long! Ha, ha, ha!" I reach up and rake my nails across his face as hard as I can.

"Aaarrgghh! The bear still has claws I see!" He backhands me, and I lie still.

"Leave her Captain! She'll soon be dead and we will carry her corpse to Queen Devona. Let's find something to eat and return in the morning. With the river flooding and her bleeding out, she won't get far. Tracking her will give the boys some practice, and then we can gut her."

He did not know how his bitter words allowed me to reach to my soul's depths and scrape the last of my strength, but soon he would.

When all is quiet, I force myself to my knees and then painfully slowly to stand. I cannot remove the arrow, but I can close the wound. I break the exposed shaft and channel heat to my hands so I can cauterize the opening in my back. This child *will* live! He will know his lineage and his destiny. I will do whatever it takes to make sure of it.

I stumble in the dark until I come to a village. Most of the doors are shut for the night. Firelight glows from windows where families gather safe and warm. I use my sight to find one with a cold hearth. I find it on the outskirts of the village, but just as I'm heading for it, movement catches my eye. A woman trudges to open the front door of a nearby cottage carrying a heavy pail. In the moonlight her silhouette shows a belly just as large as mine. I whisper a silent thanks to The One and make my way to her shed. I hide there until morning, clenching every muscle to hold tightly onto the life within me. When the woman finally rouses to start her morning, she finds me lying on the shed floor.

I speak my first words in nine months. "Please do not be alarmed." I am surprised at the strength of my voice given my current state. "Despite how I must look to you, I am Alanna Bear-Claw, and I need you to write these words down."

"Oh Mistress! I will get help! Please wait here!"

She turns to leave, but I thrust out a hand and grip her wrist with a strength I did not know I possessed. "There is no time! Listen to me, please." I can feel my abdomen hardening and clench my teeth from the pain.

"Yes Mistress, but no pen or paper is needed. I was born a scribe, a power my family has deemed useless. Perhaps the fates knew you would have need of me."

"Praise The One! Look on me and record what is said, then scribe."

I recount every detail I can for my unborn child. Everything about his father and my love for him, our hopes and dreams; our beliefs and our betrayal, and when I am done, I sleep.

"Mistress you must wake up! Oh, please, please wake up!"

"What is your name, Child?"

"Oh, thank the heavens! I am Wleia."

"Wleia, you carry twins."

"You are blessed with the sight Mistress? Are they well, my babies? I have not felt movement in some time and am most worried."

"Wleia, one child is no more and the other struggles. I am sorry."

"Oh Elrond! Have mercy! What am I to do?"

"Wleia, peace Child, peace! How much longer before it is your time to deliver?"

"The midwife says I have several more weeks. I only look further along because I carry two."

"That is good. The violence of the last few weeks has brought my time too early, and my child is not yet ready. Wleia, you will not like what I suggest, but it is the only way to save your remaining child... and mine. You know who I am and what I am capable of?" Wleia nods despite the tears streaming down her face. "I will perform a spell and place my child in your womb, and your deceased child in mine. Do you understand?" She can only nod in open-mouthed shock. "It will be painful and it *will* kill me in the process, but I am dead already. In my pack you will find some jewelry, use it to provide for my... our family. Can you read?" Again a slight nod is the response, "Very good, take this list and now you must hurry! Gather these ingredients and return by sunset."

Wleia did all I asked and at sunset we sit, arm in arm, belly to belly, mother to mother.

"Flesh to flesh, let the two joined be irrevocably meshed. Womb to tomb, life for death and death for life." A ripping can be felt and as one, we scream. I sink onto the bed of straw and with my last sight, see two heartbeats in the womb of the woman called Wleia.

Chapter 3

"PUSH WLEIA! PUSH WOMAN!"

"Arrrgggg!"

"Waaaahhh! Waaahhh!"

"Ahh, you have two beautiful children Wleia, a son and a daughter. Your daughter's lungs are strong, but your son is very quiet. And he has a strange mark on him."

"Give them to me, please. Thank you for your help. I left your payment in the front room. Be well."

"And you too, be well."

As she glanced down at her children, she brought her daughter close to let her nurse. She knew immediately the boy child was not her own. He had a healed scar running across his body from shoulder to hip, and he stared at her with knowledge and understanding, from piercing steel gray eyes.

Once her daughter had fallen asleep, she took the other baby in her arms.

"Prince Alric, I am your mother now and will love you as such. I believe you know the truth if you are as... she was. You are safe now, and safe will you stay for as long as I can make it so."

And he let loose a cry that tore her heart in two. It was not the cry of a newborn, but of a child grieving his mother. She nursed him and he went to sleep beside his sister Elainea, holding her hand.

16 years later

"Alric, if you don't leave me alone, I will scream so loud your eardrums will shatter into a million pieces and pierce that stupid little brain of yours!"

"Sure thing Laney." Alric grinned broadly as he watched his sister back away from him and the pail of water levitating between them.

"Mother told you to water the herb garden, go away!"

"Well, she always says you grow like a weed, so I'm still being obedient."

Elainea opened her mouth to scream, and not a sound came out. She glared at her brother realizing he had placed a small barrier over her mouth as he upended the bucket over her red hair, but not a drop touched her. A red haze surrounded her, turning the water to mist.

"See, I only wanted to help you practice your gifts Sister. You rely solely on your voice too much."

"Your concern is touching Brother," Elainea said as she stormed away.

Twins as different as night and day in looks as well as talents. That is what everyone believed. Elainea, could control fire to a degree and projected her voice to levels with such precision and clarity, it could be lethal. While Alric could form barriers and control objects with his mind. Both youths were stronger than most, and therefore, were outcasts among their peers. When their powers became evident at a very young age, Wleia used the last of the money left by Alanna to move them from the village. To protect them and herself she had gone as far as hiring a mage to change the color of her eyes and hair. They now lived on a small farm near the river, in the shadow of the great mountains.

"Children! Come inside for supper!" Wleia watched from the doorway as they ran toward her. These were her children, and her heart trembled within her. They would be sixteen tomorrow. Where had time gone? Elainea was of marriageable age, and Alric could be conscripted into King David's army. Mere children, and yet so much could and would be asked of them. Even so, she would not alter a single moment from that fateful night to now. "Come, we will celebrate tonight. We have honey cakes and roast lamb for everyone."

"Really Mother? Honey cakes! I knew you loved me more than that rude brother of mine."

"Hush, I have candied dates as well."

"Ha! Sister, we are both loved."

They playfully jostled each other through the door and to the table.

"Come, let us give thanks for what we are about to receive." Once they had finally settled Wleia began. "We give all thanks and praise to The One, the giver of life, the bringer of harvest, the provider and protector of our lives. We humbly seek Your blessing this night over this meal, and over the lives of these two children as they enter adulthood." The siblings shared a confused glance at each other over their clasped hands. "Guide them, oh wise Father, toward their destiny. Reveal their paths, strengthen them, fill them with your power. Use them for your greater good. Iwe hivyo."

"Iwe hivyo," the twins repeated.

Silence filled the small room after the unusual prayer.

"Mother..." Alric started.

"Shh... I will explain after we eat. Now eat my children, eat."

All was almost forgotten over the succulent lamb and sweetness of the dates and honey cakes, but every so often the twins would catch the other's eye with an obvious question. What was that all about?

Chapter 4

LATER THAT NIGHT, after the dishes were washed, the small family sat by the fire. Wleia sat in the chair with her two children at her knees, as they had for so many nights over the years. However, this night would change everything for all of them.

"My loves, I would shield you from the entire world if I could. Tomorrow, you turn sixteen and things will change for you. Normally, your gifts would not have manifested until now so I always knew you both were different, stronger. We don't know what will change tomorrow, maybe nothing, maybe everything? One, give me strength."

"Mother, what is wrong? You have never worked yourself into such a state before. We are always careful to restrain our abilities in public. Please, calm yourself. You are scaring Elainea. You know how weak her constitution is." Alric said with a laugh.

"Why you wretch. You never could stay serious for too long. I am made of stronger stuff than you!" Elainea retorted with a slap to the side of her brother's arm.

"Enough!" Never had their mother shouted at them, and the shock had both their jaws clicking shut with eyes quickly downcast. "My loves, forgive me. Please, now is not the time for joking. What I am about to tell you is hard, the hardest! But I made a vow sixteen years ago, Alric, a vow to... Alanna Bear-Claw."

"What? You knew her? That's amazing! We have heard stories of her and King Kaison's betrayal. She was the high priestess and queen! Why have you never told us? I can understand not telling anyone else, given the current regime, but us Mother?" Alric was in shock.

"You will understand in the end, my son. My gifts as a scribe, working for various businessmen, have provided well for us. However, there is one event that I have held onto until now. Alric this is more for you than Elainea, but you both have need of the information. Come, grasp my hands.”

As the three held hands, Wleia’s eyes went white and the vision was played in the minds of her children as if they were there.

A woman lying prostrate in the forest raked her nails across a soldier’s face before staggering into a dark barn, finally collapsing on some straw. A tattered tunic wrapped around her hunched shoulders, her bronze hair loosely flowing around her head. But the strength in her gray eyes was piercing.

“I, Alanna Bear-Claw, high priestess of The One and Queen of Elhaanai, charge you, Wleia Mwandishi, with this oath and task. You will raise my son Alric Bear-Claw as your own. You will hide these truths from him until his sixteenth year, at which time, he must journey to the great mountain and seek Shama the High Priest; there, he will begin instruction on how to reclaim the throne. My son, I am sorry I will not be there to meet you, to love you. But know this, you are flesh of my flesh, bone of my bone and I love you with every fiber of my being. I have fought for you and I have died for you, *you will live*! And if you have any of your father in you, which I believe you must, you won’t be able to stay serious for more than a few moments at a time, even in light of such a discovery as this. Let that humor see you through what is to come. How I loved him. How he loved you. He named you Alric. Be the noble leader he knew you would become. I do not know what the kingdom will look like when your time comes, but I do know you will be equipped for the journey.

“Wleia, I am sorry to place this burden on you. Your daughter will be an integral part of this journey. In what capacity, I know not. But they must travel together. Be strong and courageous my love. I am ever in your blood and in your heart. Remember who and whose you are.”

The vision faded from view.

“I don’t understand.” Alric looked heartbroken.

“Sixteen years ago your true mother stumbled into my barn. Wounded, near death, and bearing you in her womb. She begged me to scribe for her that message and then did the unbelievable. You see,” she glanced at Elainea who had remained silent. “I was carrying twins, but I hadn’t felt any movement in days. Thank The One,

Alanna was gifted with sight and told me I had lost one child and the other was barely clinging to life. She offered me the chance to save you both, and I took it. She performed a spell, and switched you, Alric, with my lost baby. Guards came the following day, having tracked her scent with hounds. They took her body away and declared both she and the child dead. I carried you both for a few more weeks and delivered. When your gifts developed early, we moved from my hometown here to the edge of Egon, I could not risk anyone wondering how you were so powerful. It is also why I changed my hair and eye color Elainea, not vanity. I had to do everything I could so guards would never look at me and remember what role I played that night. And here we are." The silence was deafening, each lost in their own thoughts.

"Mother, are there any more candied dates?"

Elainea playfully smacked Alric across the back of his head.

"What? I'm hungry and what can we do Sister?" In a rare show of seriousness, Alric locked eyes, first with Wleia and then Elainea. "You are my mother and you are my sister. However and why fate saw to bring us together, here we are. Tomorrow will bring what it does, and we will deal with it as we have with everything else, as a family."

Chapter 5

THE NEXT MORNING DAWNED CLEAR, the Cerulean sky didn't have a cloud in sight and the river lay like glass, but inside the small home, everything was changing. Alric lay on his bed as if in a coma. His eyes clouded over, lost in sight. Objects from around his room floated in the air on unseen currents. On the other side of the home, Elainea hovered over her bed. Her hair had turned a more vibrant shade of red, and her lips rapidly formed silent words, while vines wrapped themselves around her bedpost as if reaching for her.

Wleia sat in the main room before the cold hearth and repeated her prayers to The One for guidance and protection. Suddenly, a wind blew through the room with such force that the door and all the windows were flung open. Wleia threw herself to the floor and covered her head in fear.

Across the kingdom, another door was flung open, but not by the gale force of rising power. No, this door flew open from rage.

"AAAKKKRRROOONNNIIIUUUSSS!" Queen Devona screamed the name of the captain of the guard as loud as she could.

"Yes Mistress?" He said, eyes wide above the claw marks scarring his features.

"Sixteen years ago, you brought me the body of my sister-in-law and her unborn child, did you not?" she asked him, while walking slowly to where he stood, just inside the door.

"Yes Mistress."

"Then why do the winds change? Why do the Oracles grin into their bowls? Why does the child live?" The last part was said so quietly, he barely heard her, but he felt fatality in her words.

"I... I... I... don't know, Mistress! She had not given birth. The arrow pierced her from her back and through her belly. We saw with our own eyes the lifeless male child cut from her womb. I swear it! She was found in the barn of a widow."

"A simple widow? There must have been a reason, beside safety, that she hid in that barn. Alanna never did anything without cause. THINK!"

Akronius thought for a moment and then he visibly swallowed. "She was… the widow… she was…" Akronius felt a tremor run through his body at the thought of the repercussions that were sure to follow after he said the next word.

"SHE, WAS, WHAT?" Devona pronounced each word as if they were daggers that could pierce him.

"Pregnant." Akronius could not look Devona in the eye. He knew he had made a potentially fatal mistake.

Devona was silent and did not even blink as she processed what he had said. Then all hell broke loose with the shrill scream she let out. "AAAHHHH! What did you say? Why wasn't I told this years ago? You knew as well as I, she was a high priestess and capable of any number of spells! Including, transference! You idiot! You, useless piece of slime! Find her, find that woman or I will rip your still-beating heart from your chest! GO!"

Her screams followed Akronius to the barracks where he formed a party of his best men to track down this woman.

Chapter 6

"MOTHER?" WLEIA'S PRAYERS WERE interrupted by her daughter. "Mother, why do you cry?" It is alright. I, we are alright."

She had not heard the steps of her child, so, when she looked up, she could not stifle the gasp that escaped. Elainea looked ethereal. Her hair was brighter, and seemed to hold fire within each strand. She stood straight with a confidence she did not possess yesterday. And just as silently, her son, Alric floated into the room. His eyes had always been a dull gray, but now they looked like molten silver, and a current seemed to skim just over the surface of his skin barely discernible, but there all the same.

Wleia's eyes widened even further until…

"Ha, ha, ha! Mother you should see the look on your face! I doubt your eyes could have gotten any larger!" Both children collapsed in a fit of giggles.

"Why you rotten pair of tomatoes!" The family laughed together and the tension of the new day broke. Chores were completed and breakfast prepared. As the trio sat around the table, they could feel the shift in the atmosphere as Alric began to speak.

"Mother, you know I am not one for serious talk and though I mocked it earlier, I have changed. I can feel power coursing within me with no outlet. I can… see things I do not understand. Like, those seeds you think are pumpkin are actually squash seeds and will grow to be quite large if you let them. That the cow will give birth to a bull, and that the goat will soon die. I also know soldiers are looking for you… for me." The latter part was said solemnly, almost a whisper, without meeting anyone's eye.

"That is to be expected." Wleia sighed. "They do not know your name, but will be looking for a boy your age with silver eyes. The fact that everyone thinks you are a twin will only provide temporary protection." She turned to look at Elainea.

"And you, Love?"

"I can feel the heat pooling in my stomach. I can *see* sound all around me; each step, each breath and flutter of a butterfly wing. I can silence it or amplify it. I can sense things as well, plants, herbs and words. Spells are flowing through my mind like...like... I don't know. Like I've always known them."

Wleia looked at her children with amazement and pride. Yes, The One had equipped them for this journey and she would not hold them back, no matter the cost.

♔

Devona paced back and forth before the fireplace in her war room. It had once been the bedroom of her brother and his wife. The secret passageway she had found here, proved useful. Treachery could come from anyone. She should know. The door opened and in strutted her son, David.

"Mother, why so worried? I'm sure our men will find that hag and my cousin mucking out a stall somewhere in the backwoods. There is no reason he would know his lineage. Alanna was on the run and almost dead. The spell you suspect her to have used would have killed her quickly." He bit into an apple and finding it less than perfect, tossed the remainder into the flames.

Devona stared at him with thinly veiled disgust as he examined his teeth in the small glass, he always carried with him. She'd had such high hopes for him. He was born under the right stars, carried the right blood within him, and yet he was useless. He had no true gifts, unless you count debauchery and greed. He spent so much time staring at his own reflection in the garden pools that it was a wonder he didn't fall in and drown. He showed no interest in ruling, he trusted her to tell him what to do. At least he was obedient.

"David, your aunt was many things but weak was never one of them. Even in her dying, I am confident she found a way to leave a message for your cousin, informing him of everything." Devona walked to her desk and glanced at the maps strewn there. There was still so much to accomplish. In disposing of her brother, she was able to broker alliances with the neighboring lands, Arcana and

Vimeo. Both had been enemies in the past due to one's allegiance to the dark lord and the other's refusal to believe in anything other than themselves. But the past was past, a new future was ripe for the taking and Devona planned to take as much as she could.

A knock sounded at the door. "Your Majesties, Lord Vicrano requests an audience," a messenger announced.

"See him to the throne room!" Devona could not stand the man. Years ago, he had met with King Kaison and requested a marriage between David and his daughter Sybella, to join the two nations as one. Arcana was a port city on the other side of the mountain and would have brought great trade to their lands. Of course, Kaison refused, citing the worship of the dark lord would corrupt his people, despite the financial advantage it would bring them. The fool placed too much importance on The One.

After their meeting, she had met with Lord Vicrano secretly.

"My Lord, forgive the interruption, I know you are preparing to leave. I overheard your conversation with my brother and greatly disagree with the outcome."

Lord Vicrano looked the woman over and recognizing a kindred spirit, he smiled. "Do you? And what good does your disagreement do me? You are no one of import." That his comment had hit its intended mark was obviously written on my face.

"I could become someone of great importance in the future, if I were certain of your allegiance and promise of marriage between our children. My son shows great promise and I hear your girl studies in the black temple to become a priestess one day."

"You hear correctly. Alright, you have my word, should the opportunity present itself."

Chapter 7

DEVONA QUICKLY CHANGED INTO a gilded robe and placed the crown on her head. Its weight brought a smile to her lips; she never tired of wearing it. Strolling slowly into the throne room, she stepped lightly. From the shadows she was able to observe Lord Vicrano who stood at the window, arms clasped behind his back. But his hands were clasped tightly, knuckles white. He was anxious today. She had managed to avoid setting an actual date for the wedding for two years; perhaps he was tired of waiting.

"Lord Vicrano, greetings. To what do I owe this visit?"

"Devona, I come with my sincerest apologies. My daughter has run off and married some... some... scoundrel without my knowledge or consent! She knew of the arranged marriage and I had hoped to..."

"My lord, my lord, do not trouble yourself." Devona practically cooed. She couldn't have been happier. "Children will be children after all. We can only try to guide them toward the right path. However, I do not believe you would come all this way simply to be the bearer of bad news. I know you far better than that."

"You are right. I come with a possible solution to the change to the expected course of events. We do not necessarily need a marriage, we understand each other well enough, I believe. However, we are in need of new blood. The seafaring life is a rough one, and we lose many Arcanan men to its waves. We have plenty of women, young and old alike, and you have an army of virile men with no wars to fight. Let us unite on a broader scale."

Devona walked over to her throne and sat, this was not the first time he had suggested this, and she couldn't help but wonder at the timing. Light and dark never mixed evenly, one would always overpower the other. How could she make sure things tilted in her favor?

"What do you suggest, my lord?"

"Remove the ban on our citizens settling in either region. We will construct a bridge over the river and a road around the mountain to our ports, making it safe for travel in both directions. You will provide the wood and we the labor. No longer will the sea be our only means of trade. You will have access to our lands, our goods and the regions beyond us."

Ahh, now we get to it, she thought. *He will have full control of my ability to pass through his lands to conquer those beyond. He knows my ambitions and would use them against me. To the east of us is the sea, and if I ever desire to cross it, I would need his ships and captains. To the west is desert. I have no desire to explore the barren wasteland. To the south lie our sister cities, Elhasheda and Elphanuel. Neither poses a threat and easily fell in line with the change in power.*

She watched him and knew he saw the wheels in her head turning. He could wait a while longer. "Let me consult my son, after all he will soon be king. I will send a missive with my... our answer."

With his mouth set in a hard line, he offered a stiff bow and walked out.

Devona went back to her war room to discuss current events with David, only to find him sound asleep in the same chair she had left him in, in the middle of the day! She chose not to wake him and instead headed to see her Oracle. "Chumbra."

"Yes, Mistress. How may I serve you today?"

"You were chosen as the new Oracle based on your affinity for the dark arts. I need you to create a spell, a solution to the deficiencies in my son. What can you offer?"

"Of course, my Queen! I knew this day would come. I took the initiative to replicate a potion that would do just what you desire. We are all born with gifts, but sadly not all of us are strong enough to awaken these traits ourselves. This is a common practice in the black temples. It is derived from the blood of a strongly gifted person and several other ingredients. Here! Have him drink this before he retires for the night and come morning he will be a new man."

Devona took the vial and examined it in the light. It was completely opaque. She assumed it would taste as vile as it looked, and wondered how she would get her son to drink it.

Devona went back to her room and not finding David there, she went on to his room. When she opened his door, she saw him sound asleep. She stood over her son, in one hand was the vial and in the other a dagger. She pressed the tip to his throat, just hard enough to wake him.

He gasped. "Wha… wha-what are you doing? Mother what is..?"

"It would be so easy for someone to slit your throat while you slept like a babe. You are so trusting. When will you have the awareness of a man? Of a king?"

She could see the moment he realized the extent of the disappointment she had in him as a son, and instead of becoming angry or indignant he wilted before her eyes. "If I were a man, I would kill you as I did your uncle and assume the throne myself!" She spat. "Here! Drink this, perhaps it will help you grow into the man you were supposed to be."

She watched him tip the vial into his mouth and grimace as he swallowed. She removed the blade and silently left the room, abandoning him to his fate. Be it life or death.

Chapter 8

THE NEXT MORNING WAS OVERCAST and Devona wondered if it was a sign of what was to come as she headed toward her son's chamber. Nuru manor was quiet in the early dawn hours and she barely wanted to breathe lest she break the silence. She stood outside his door and strained her ears to listen but heard nothing. She pushed his door open and let her eyes adjust to the gloom. No fire was lit and all the looking glasses had been covered. She wondered how he had been changed.

"David, where are you?"

"Mother."

She gasped at the prick of a blade against her throat. "Mother, your awareness is lacking."

The ice in his voice was enough to cause her flesh to pimple in alarm. He wouldn't... would he? And where did he come from? She hadn't seen him anywhere. Just as suddenly as it had appeared, the blade was gone. She whipped around and saw nothing.

"David, stop these games. Show yourself!"

"Tsk tsk tsk... temper, temper Your Majesty. Would you like to see what your ingenuity has wrought?"

She gazed around, wide-eyed, as his voice seemed to come from everywhere at once, then "BOO!" His face popped out of the darkness like a phantom and disappeared again. His raucous laughter filtered through the air like an echo, bouncing off every surface and filling her ears. She had never been afraid of her son before now. What had she created? She could feel his breath on her neck. He grazed her arm with his fingertips and then appeared in a chair that was deep in the shadows of the room.

"You see mother, I can clothe myself in darkness. I can wear the shadows as if they were a cloak. I could be right next to you, and you would never know it."

She gazed at her son in shock. More than the physical gifts he had developed, there was now darkness in his eyes. She hoped she would not live to regret this alteration. And yet, the possibilities were endless! And if he were to have a child... oh the dark lord had provided for them indeed. Much more than The One ever had.

"That is a wonderful development David. We can use this gift in any number of ways. We could spy on our allies. Travel to distant lands and learn their weaknesses before we assassinate their leaders and take over. It could all be so simple!" The more she thought about it, the more possibilities came to her.

"I will return with the Oracle. He will tell you what comes next in your training." He had said nothing the whole time, letting her plan the future as if he could care less. Then he faded back into the inky blackness of his room. If she looked hard enough, she could still see the dark glint in his eyes, like a black flame, until that too winked out. She left the room trembling, whether from excitement or fear, she did not know and refused to think too hard about it.

It hadn't been hard to feign anger over his daughter's marriage. In truth, she'd had his blessing to marry Ashrek, the son of Lord Overton of Vimeo. The man was strong, and possessed great gifts so he would father strong children. Plus, he followed behind Sybella like a lamb to the slaughter. He would be easy to manipulate through his daughter, as she was a female version of himself. They were both ambitious and cunning.

"We are done here. Gather the goods and meet me at the docks." Lord Vicrano said to his crew. He observed the market center on his way out of the city. The people appeared healthy and shopped with ease at the various shops. Jovial bartering could be heard between laughter and conversation, unlike his own town where knives were just as easily to be drawn over a misplaced step, as an unfair price. There were various stands offering every item one could imagine; fabric, utensils, medicinal supplies, forges, jewelry and even exotic animals. One thing he could say in King Kaison's favor, he had kept his people pure. His sister would be the downfall of the city, but that was not his concern. As long as his coffers increased from the tax he would place on the river crossing, and the soldiers left children behind, heading off to whatever quest the queen would send them on, he had no qualms against corrupting them. None at all.

Chapter 9

FOR TWO YEARS, with no success, Akronius and his men had visited every town in a ten-mile radius of where Alanna's body had been found. All the others had since returned to the manor except for him. This was his last stop before he too would be forced to tell the queen his search was unproductive, thereby rendering his life forfeited. He walked through the market, bypassing shops he had previously visited, his last stop was a seller of produce. He told the merchant the same story he had told all the others, that he was looking for his sister. He explained that they had fallen out over the father of her child and being the emotional woman that she was, she had run away about eighteen years ago. He wanted to make amends. Life was short, after all, and he would like to meet his niece or nephew. The merchant thought for a while and said there was a woman who had moved into an old hut down by the river a few years ago, but she had twins. Akronius thanked him and turned to go, bumping into a boy behind him, causing the goods he carried to fall to the floor.

"Watch where you're going kid!" Akronius snarled.

Just as the merchant said, "This is one of the twins Sir," but he didn't hear it.

"S…S…sorry Sir! My apologies, I was not paying attention as I was so focused on these ripe apples. The best in the country I swear. Let me buy you one." Alric felt the eyes of the man bore into him.

"No, it's alright. I've already eaten."

"Yes Sir. Umm, do you mind if I ask where you got those scars on your face? They look like they have quite a story behind them."

"A bear clawed me as I was killing it," he said with a grin. "But I have no time for stories now boy. I must be on my way." He rushed out of the shop without a glance back. Had he done so, he would have seen the boy watching him with an expression of rage.

"Who was that man?" Alric asked the merchant.

"A traveler looking for his long-lost sister, if he is to be believed. But between you and me, there are whispers Queen Alanna's child lives and Devona seeks him out to finish the task she started years ago. Nasty business if you ask me. My bones tell me, we are in for dark days ahead my boy, dark days indeed."

"You are an Oracle?"

"Not strong enough for the royals, but my gifts see me through the harvest. They reveal who lies and who tells the truth. And that man, he lies, about many things."

"Interesting, well, I best be getting these back to mother. She is making us an apple pie!"

Alric walked slowly home, keeping an eye on the surrounding road, lest the soldier catch him unaware. How would he tell his sister and mother? The time had come for them to leave. Trouble had found them at last.

"Mother, I have the apples!"

"Wash them and bring them to me Alric. Elainea is off gathering herbs."

"Again? She really needs to make friends, Mother. Spending so much time in the forest can't possibly be healthy for her mental state."

"Your concern is touching as always Brother."

"Sister. I didn't see you there." Alric said with a grin as Elainea placed her basket on the table and began separating the herbs she had gathered.

Though they had grown and matured much in the two years since learning their birth story, they still shared a gentle sibling rivalry born of love and a deep trust.

"Mother, you'll never guess who I saw at the market today." Alric said, as he crunched into an apple. It wasn't quite ripe yet, but he wouldn't throw it away. If he buried the seeds, they may have an apple tree in a few years.

"I bet it was Katakana, that pretty pink haired girl you are always mooning over when you think no one is looking," Elainea whispered.

"No, and she isn't as pretty as Rolando that man who you..."

"Shut up!"

"Ha, ha, ha, no it was neither of them. I saw a man with the most interesting claw marks across his face. He said a bear clawed him as he was killing it."

Both women turned to look at him, one with shock and the other with fear.

"You must leave." Wleia said softly. "We put it off as long as possible, but we all knew this day would come." She looked her children in the eye and sighed deeply. "Come, let us eat. Then we will speak of your journey."

"Now, there are no maps that will lead you to the temple where Shama lives. It has only been by word of mouth that anyone has ever found him. And even then, those who find him rarely come back the same way and are forbidden from speaking of the route and what they found. They come back stronger and wiser than when they left. What we do know is that you must journey to the mouth of Spyre river, where it flows down from the mountain. There you will find your next clue, and at each juncture there will be another clue to guide you further along. The mountain is treacherous and unforgiving. Do not grow careless or over confident. The weather can change in an instant and thieves from Arcana and Vimeo are known to hide in its crevices, like the roaches they are."

"We will be careful, mother. There are so many supplies we will need. Alric's belly alone will require ten packs of food!"

"You speak truth Sister. But I am a growing boy, you are stunted and don't need as much sustenance."

"Oh, you two. I pray you retain that sense of lightheartedness; it may serve you in ways you don't imagine. You won't need to pack so much food, I know it is not your favorite, but we have plenty of dried fruit and meat. You are both avid hunters, source from the land, but kill only what you will need for that day. And cover your trail as much as possible. We have much to do in the coming days."

Chapter 10

EVERY DAY WAS FILLED WITH an undercurrent of fear. Would they be discovered today? They packed slowly so as not to raise awareness. Nothing was as suspicious as buying large amounts of supplies and disappearing in the night. On each visit, they went to different merchants. They took care to always speak loudly enough to be heard about going to visit family here or there, but never the same place. If anyone looked for them, they would get conflicting information, which would throw the hounds off for a little while at least. Finally, all was gathered and the time for departure had come. The mood was somber during that last meal, none of the usual banter between the siblings. Sad smiles passed around like a bitter cup of gall.

"Children it will turn out alright. Think of it as a grand adventure. You'll get to see and experience things beyond my wildest dreams. And then you will come back. And we will see what The One has in store for us then. Let us take each day one step at a time."

Elainea threw herself across her mother's lap in anguish. "Oh Mother, Mother! I can't bear to be parted from you, I can't! What if our training takes years? What if you are sick while I am away? Who will care for you? What if... what if you..." Tears tracked down her cheeks, saying what her lips could not.

"What if I die?" Wleia said. She placed one finger under her daughter's chin and raised it. "We will all die my love. It's only a matter of when and how. I am an old woman now, nearing my fiftieth year. But I will do my best not to place any added risks to rush into that eventuality."

The women hugged each other tightly. Wleia looked over the head of one child into the piercing gray eyes of the other and they exchanged a subtle nod. He would watch over her with everything he had.

The following morning, the three of them stood arm in arm, Wleia in the middle, facing the mountain. The tops of which were snowcapped, and enveloped by rolling clouds.

"You can do this. The One has gifted you with the strength to accomplish anything. Within each of you lies a well of untapped potential, listen for the small voice giving you direction. Trust it. Trust each other. Despite the situation surrounding your birth, you are true siblings. Born together from my womb, passed through the same water. Alric, you were wounded when you came to me, I can only assume that some of your blood transferred to your sister resulting in the strength she possesses and a bond similar to soul mates. I know you can communicate without words; in some supernatural way you can anticipate each other. You probably never even noticed, it was just natural to you, but I did. You will need to rely on that bond. I will be praying for you night and day. And should I not be here in body when you return, know I am with you always in spirit. Now go. Do not look back. Look for the markers set in stone. They will lead you to Shama. Be strong and courageous my loves!"

The twins clasped hands for a moment, before quickly letting go, preferring to bump shoulders. Their journey into the unknown was just beginning; the voice of their mother echoing in their ears, her love pushing them forward like the wind.

Wleia stood on the river bank for as long as she could, until her children were dots on the horizon, out of sight. And then she collapsed to the soil with all the anguish she had built up over the last few days. Sobs dredged up from the depths of her soul, grief so thick it was almost tangible, so heavily weighed, that she was unable to stand under it. She grabbed fistfuls of grass and dirt as if trying to ground herself from floating away on the endless wave of pain. She felt a breeze across the back of her neck as a small voice whispered to her, 'strong and courageous,' bringing with it a peace that settled over her like a warm cloak; soothing the hollow ache in her chest. Her sobs subsided, and she sat up with a shudder. Her red rimmed eyes still turned to the mountains. She wiped her face with her apron. She could not ask of them what she was unwilling to be herself. The

One had affirmed this. She would be 'Strong and Courageous.' She would see this through to the very end.

Chapter 11

AS SHE TURNED TO LEAVE, a sound drew her to the river's edge. As she got nearer, her eyes widened in shock, behind some brambles lay a wolf, arrows protruding from its bleeding side. It struggled to rise but failed. A low growl turned into a whimper of pain. "Peace, wolf. I mean you no harm. You must be the chicken thief the merchants were recently complaining about. I am sorry to see you injured, but not so much, you understand."

Wleia spoke as if the creature could understand her. *The twins have not been gone a day and already I am speaking to animals*, she thought to herself. She could see its breathing was labored and knew it would not survive the night. She would have a wolf pelt to warm her old bones and a story to tell the children when they returned.

She sat with the wolf until its last breath, after all, no one deserved to die alone. And yet, she still heard a whimper. Looking around she spotted its source and smiled, there behind a bush was a small cub. Probably the runt of the litter, a year old at best. Its amber eyes seemed to glow in the fading sunlight and it trembled from fear.

Wleia approached the animal slowly, and let it sniff her outstretched hand. She smiled when it gave her palm a gentle lick. "Come Pup, you need warm milk and I have an empty home. You and I are going to survive." She carried the pup into the house and set it by the fire with a bowl of cow's milk. She then went outside and skinned the mother wolf. In life as in death, nothing was wasted. She set the pelt to dry and buried the carcass.

"What shall we call you Pup?" She watched it sleep after it had licked the bowl dry. As it rolled over, she realized it was a female. "Your name is Naia, you will be my comfort during this time." Sometime during the night, when the fire had turned to glowing embers, Naia crawled into Wleia's bedroom and managed to pull herself up onto the bed where she draped herself over Wleia's feet. She observed the old woman for a few moments before tucking her snout beneath her tail and closing her eyes with a sigh.

♛

Akronius spent a month in Egon. Every day, he visited another house, while every evening, he sat in the tavern and listened for anything that might help him in his search. Late one afternoon he finally heard it.

"I heard the twins left a few days ago, Shmuel. Whatever will you do with all those pastries now? That boy frequented your shop almost daily and could eat enough for two grown men! Ha, ha, ha." One villager laughed with another.

"I guess I'll have to sell them all to you, as often as your wife is angry with you, you'll need all the sweet treats you can carry!" Both men laughed and ordered another round of foaming mugs from the waitress as she passed by.

"I never understood why we call them twins. They look nothing alike, one with eyes like steel, and hair blacker than midnight. The other seemingly born of fire, with flaming-red hair. My son was quite smitten with her. He was always going on about her blue eyes." The waitress said, before heading off to get the men their drinks.

Akronius felt like someone had punched him in the chest. *The boy*! Thinking back to his encounter at the market he realized the boy had silver eyes! He had been so focused on his task that he had not seen what was right in front of him. He got up so quickly that he knocked his cup over and all eyes turned to him, but he was already half-way through the door. He had observed the family several times from afar and ruled them out based on the sole fact that they were twins. But now, he wasn't so sure. He would visit the woman at first light and find the truth.

Wleia went about her morning chores in silent prayer for her children. Out of the corner of her eye she spotted Naia creeping toward the edge of the house and then she pounced. Up flew a butterfly. Wleia chuckled to herself. The pup had much to learn, but it would be fun to watch the process. Suddenly the pup's ears went

37

straight up along with her hackles. She scampered over to Wleia a low growl coming from her throat. Her eyes trained on the nearby tree line.

Wleia squinted and shielded her eyes with her hand but barely managed to make out the silhouette of a man, possibly a soldier, by the looks of him. He slowly emerged and headed toward them. He was armed and walked with a confidence forged from many battles. When he was close enough, he called a greeting,

"Good morning to you."

"Good morning to you, Sir. What brings you so far from the village?"

"I heard you made the best apple pie in the county and just had to see for myself."

"I am flattered. Sadly, I have no apples at hand and no pies made. Perhaps if you give me some notice of the next time you'll be passing through, I can leave one for you." He was close enough now that she could see the scars across his face, and it caused her heart to skip a beat.

"That is a shame. I was so looking forward to it." He spared a quick glance at the wolf by her feet, its eyes never left his face. Akronius didn't attempt to hide his casual observation of her land and home.

"Nice place you got here by the river. Bit large to maintain by yourself, now your children are gone." He saw a tiny tick by her eye, and smiled. "I could go for a bit of fishing. Would you mind my staying on for a few days? I'd pay you of course, and help around the place if you needed it."

"Why of course you can. What a kind gesture, offering to help an old woman in her hour of need. My children have gone off to visit family in the south for the winter. I am too old for the journey now."

He was surprised by her willingness to share information, and though he tried to hide the shock from reaching his face, from her smile, he could tell he had failed.

"Come, you can start at once. I need water drawn from the river. The pail gets so heavy. My son Al...Alton, Al for short, usually does it for me. I just used the last of what he gathered this morning.

The One must have sent you to help me. I also need some wood chopped, eggs gathered and the cow needs milking. You mentioned fishing? Be sure to bring some for a meal tonight. What did you say your name was Son?"

He watched her with wide eyes and a slack jaw, "Uhhh, my name is Akronius."

"Nice to meet you. You should get going, the day has started without us, the sun will be setting before you know it and it is getting colder every day. Go on now young man, go on."

She handed him a large pail and turned to go into the house. The wolf cub stayed by the door watching him with amber eyes.

Wleia watched the man from the window, her heart racing within her chest. *Keep your friends close*, she thought, *and your enemies closer*. She closed her eyes and said a quick prayer for wisdom and protection then set about lighting a fire to cook a light meal for two.

Akronius was baffled as he lowered the pail into the river. For the life of him he couldn't understand why the woman had agreed to his offer. If she were hiding the location of the heir to the throne she would have refused, wouldn't she? Maybe she was more cunning than he gave her credit for. Maybe she actually knew nothing. In either case, he had room and board for now. He would use the time to see what information he could gather.

Chapter 12

FURTHER DOWN THE VALLEY, the siblings followed the Spyre river as they had been instructed to.

"Alric, what do you think we will find once we reach the end of the river?"

"I have no idea, really. I suppose we will find a marker of some sort that will tell us where to go from that point. According to mother, at least."

"I just wish we had more information to go on. There are so many unknowns waiting for us."

"I agree with you there, but in the meantime, we can practice our gifts. Maybe then we will be prepared enough for whatever the priest will throw at us. We have traveled far enough for today. Let's camp and try to find something to eat." Alric set about finding kindling for a fire while Elainea looked through the pack for flints.

"Alric, didn't you pack the flints?"

"No, I thought you did."

"I can't believe you! Even in the face of challenges such as these you cannot be trusted. Now what will we do without the ability to make a fire?" Elainea complained. She looked over at her brother with frustration only to find him smiling at her. "You forgot them on purpose, didn't you?"

"Sister, what need do we have of flints when you are here? Come on, light the fire for us. I know you can do it. Just think of how annoying I can be," he said with a smirk.

Elainea looked at the pile of kindling with trepidation. Could she do it? She had never attempted to start a fire before, at least not intentionally. Several accidents had occurred over the years when she lost her temper.

"Perhaps it will help if you close your eyes and try to feel the fire. Listen to the sound of my voice." She closed her eyes obediently, the reluctance still evident on her face. "Picture the fire inside of you. It is part of you, it is yours to command. Now, pull a small part of that fire to the front of your mind. See it in front of you, feel its warmth. Now, open your eyes."

Elainea opened her eyes to find a single flickering tear-shaped flame hovering over the kindling. She gazed at it in wonder and then directed it lower until it touched the wood and caught. Her jaw dropped as she realized that she had done it. Despite the fact that she was sweating from the effort it had taken, she was immensely proud of herself. She raised her eyes to her brother in gratitude. Only the moment was ruined when he said, "See, I'm always right. You should listen to me more often." She wanted to throw him in the river.

"Well, oh powerful one, since you know so much. How about you find us some meat to roast over this fire?"

"It would be my pleasure." Alric walked over to the river as Elainea watched from the camp. He raised his hands over the river and bubbles of water floated toward him. Elainea started to laugh at him, teasing him that they could not eat water, when she noticed that within each bubble swam a fish. Of course, he just had to prove her wrong. As he turned toward her, she could see his arms trembling from the exertion and knew he was having just as much trouble controlling his gifts as she had with the fire. He dropped his arms with a groan causing the bubbles to burst and the fish to fall, flopping about on the ground. He gave her a sheepish look as he bent to retrieve them.

"We have much work to do to master these gifts, Laney," he said softly

"Yes, we do," she agreed as she skewered one of the fish and set it atop the blaze. "But master them we shall."

Devona barely had enough time to leap out of the way, as for the third time this week David sent another Oracle storming from his room, because of his trickery. He had shirked his duty before his gifts manifested, and now he did the same only in a grander and far

scarier fashion. He had taken to roaming the halls and hiding himself in the most unexpected places. Every shadow and dimly lit corner became his playground. He hid in empty chambers for the inhabitants to return and then tortured them throughout the night, whispering and howling like a wraith. He refused to reveal himself to his tutors, instead speaking from his cloak of darkness, moving from place to place, his voice surrounding them, his eyes alone watching them from shadows. He used knives, sticks and any sharp object he could find to poke unsuspecting people as they went about their duties. Everyone in the manor was carrying torches to dispel the darkness during the day and they barely slept at night.

"David, must you terrorize every tutor I manage to convince to come here? Even if you were a child, these pranks would scarcely be tolerated and you are a grown *man*. They do speak amongst themselves and soon no one will want to set eyes on you, let alone try to train you. You must…"

"I *must* nothing!" He interrupted her. "You created me in more ways than one, Mother. Do you now regret it? Giving me life and life again? I think I will stop taking orders from you. I am to be king, actually I *am* the king. From this day forward you will do as I say. Do you understand Mother? We shall make it official, tomorrow will be my coronation." There was a manic glint in his eye and spittle formed at the corner of his mouth. He stalked closer to her, hands opening and closing as if he could feel her throat beneath his palms. The veins in his neck and forehead pulsed and his face took on a mottled look.

"I don't hear you Mother," he said in a sing-song voice.

"Yes David."

"WHAT DID YOU CALL ME?" He bellowed.

"Y… yes, King David." Devona spat out through gritted teeth.

"Better, much better. Now go tell the cook to prepare a grand feast. Tomorrow, I will become King!"

Chapter 13

LORD VICRANO WALKED INTO HIS manor and was greeted with the clamor of nails against granite. His hounds careened toward him at a reckless speed. He whistled sharply and they skidded to a halt, barely an inch from his feet.

"Good dogs." Now if only everyone could be trained to be just as obedient. "Where is your mistress?" He walked through the halls, neither glancing to the left or right, for he already knew where he would find his daughter.

"How long have you locked yourself away in my study, Daughter? You are wed now; you have other obligations than just the advancement of our borders. I need a strong grandson."

"Father, welcome back. I trust you were successful?" Sybella inquired without even looking up to acknowledge her father's presence or the statement he had made. She had no intention of bearing a child until it was in *her* best interest, which was one thing she had full control over. Had the snub been done by anyone else, their eyes would have been melted within their skulls. Father could control the temperature of any object, animate and otherwise. And he operated with precision, as he did in all things. You did not want to be on the receiving end of his focused glare, she had the scars to prove it.

"That woman is insufferable." Vicrano said as he inspected the maps strewn across the table. "She gave me the run around for years, hoping that sniveling brat of hers would grow up to be a worthy match for you, and I went right along with it for no reason other than to build trust. And now, she must 'consult' him since he is destined to be king. That boy will never be king, and even if he does assume the throne, she will be the one pulling his strings."

"So be it Father, we will bide our time as agreed upon. Let her run her people into the ground, they will be ripe for us to pick, like the persimmons you are so fond of." She said this in a monotone, matter of fact voice. This was why he trusted her, she was pragmatic and cunning, but could flip the besotted female act on in the blink of an eye.

"Speaking of strong children, Father, I have a gift for you."

Vicrano looked at his daughter in bewilderment, "Oh really, what is it?"

"Alcherist was experiencing some misgivings about our plan. He actually thought he could close his borders, and instructed his guards to kill anyone from our battalion on sight. We proved no one is untouchable." She walked over to a basket in the corner of the room as she spoke. When she turned, she carried a child in her arms and a wicked grin on her face. "Lucky for us, no one knows of my gift and I was able to pop in rather unannounced and leave with this small token. Isn't he precious?"

"Ahh, you have mastered the art of warfare very well Daughter. We will hold the child until they come to their senses. For now, we must turn our sights to more menial tasks. I do not plan to wait on the approval of Devona for the pass. Have our men begin construction immediately in both locations. Devona will hope to control the pass, we will let her think she does, whilst we have the secondary route locked for our purposes."

Vicrano pointed on the map to where he planned to construct both roads. The main one would cross the mouth of the river and skirt around the base of the mountain range to the port. The hidden one on the other hand would be more direct and inherently more dangerous as it would be cut directly through the mountain. This latter part would not even be possible had it not been for the gift Ashrek possessed to manipulate earth and rock.

"Once we have the tunnel complete, we will have illusions placed for concealment, and we can begin part two."

Now that the wailing had finally subsided, a desolate silence filled the halls of Utata manor where Lord Alcherist lived with his wife, Elmeera. Barely two months ago, they had been filled with cheers and joyful laughter at the birth of his son, Khal. They had tried to conceive for five long years. He was their miracle. From whom he could not say, he and his people did not swear allegiance to The One nor to the dark lord. They believed that hard work and perseverance could produce whatever you needed, and if it didn't... then it didn't, move on. His neighbors to the south, light followers as they were called in Vimeo, believed The One provided for all their needs. He was believed to be all-powerful, all-knowing, all-seeing and unconditionally loving, despite anyone's shortcomings. That made little sense to Alcherist, but it was worlds better than his neighbors to the east. They believed in human sacrifices, thinking power could be found in blood, taking whatever they wanted regardless of who got hurt in the process. Unfortunately, they were also stronger, boasting a population almost triple that of Vimeo and held sole access to the ports. That was the only reason he had agreed with his brother for his nephew's marriage with that lunatic daughter of Vicrano. Lord Overton, his brother, was pleased with the arrangement. He could see the political and trade benefits it would provide for them. But when word of the meeting Vicrano had held with Devona reached Alcherist's ears, he got an inkling of the game he had entered into, unwittingly. He had tried to back out, and was now paying the price. Somehow, his son had been snatched from his cradle with no one seeing the culprit. But he knew, despite Overton thinking he was a weak man, he had little birds everywhere that whispered to him, that wicked girl had the gift of teleportation. She had simply popped in and out while everyone slept and took his child. His *son!* In the three days since his abduction, no demands had been sent. Nevertheless, he had reopened his borders to travelers and sent a missive to Vicrano asking for the return of his child. His face contorted in disgust, *asking,* for his own child back when everything in him wanted to storm their gates and burn their city to the ground! His wife would not look at him and had refused to leave her room until Khal was safely returned. He could not blame her; what kind of man was he? He sat down in his dining hall at the head of his table and looked at the empty seat to his right, the bassinet between them, lowered his head to his arms and wept.

Chapter 14

DEVONA STARED AT HER REFLECTION in the mirror. She had lost weight and there was a haunted look in her eye. She looked old, tired. She was not excluded from the torturous nightly visits from her son. But she had convinced David to postpone the coronation, claiming they needed time to let the other rulers know. He would want them present to acknowledge his rise to power. His vanity had not lessened with the awakening of his gifts and he readily agreed. But sadly, the time had come. With a deep breath she turned to exit the room.

At the other end of the manor, David paced in his chambers. He was king, *king!* All his life his mother had pestered him, nagged him, berated him, *tortured* him, wait, what? She had never tortured him, annoyed him, yes, but all mothers did that right? She had only wanted the best for him, she believed in him, had high hopes for him, too high. She was so overbearing and manipulative. From where were these thoughts coming? He ran his hands through his hair again in frustration. He didn't know his own mind! Curse her for making him drink that vile concoction! He sank into a chair with his head clasped tightly in his hands, wishing but unable to forget that night.

In the past...

He desperately wanted to cry out as the mixture slid down his throat like fire, but no sound came out. His mother removed the knife, turned her back on him and shut the door. She had abandoned him to whatever fate would have him, life or death. At that moment it felt like death was winning. He clawed at his throat, then his chest, as his body arched off the bed leaving bloody welts from his perfectly manicured nails. He curled in on himself clutching his belly in agony. He had never felt such pain! He could feel the sweat pouring off of him, soaking his bed linen. He had no concept of time as he gave in to the pain and let his eyes close under the weight of his eyelids. When he came to himself, he was lying flat, the bed sheets twisted around his torso. Slowly, he untangled himself and sat up to assess the damage. He felt the same, reaching for the mirror on his night stand, he looked the same. But he KNEW he was changed. He struggled to remember. He had had a dream and a conversation with someone that looked like him, only shrouded in darkness. He shook his head in annoyance to clear the confusion he felt. The harder he tried to remember, the foggier his mind grew, so he gave up.

The moment he did, he heard a small voice, "Welcome the darkness." He closed his eyes and dropped his chin to his chest. It was as if a switch had been flipped, he gasped and flung his head back, he could feel power flowing through his veins. It felt slimy, but thick and heavy, making him want to wipe his arms off. Everything felt so foreign, but he somehow knew what he was capable of. And then the door opened and his mother crept in. She looked around and called his name, she couldn't see him! He felt his face break into a wide smile. He crept from the bed and made his way behind her, placing a dagger at her throat like she had done to him only a few hours before He could smell her fear, actually smell it. He inhaled deeply, mmmmm it smelled delicious. After a few words and threats had been spoken between them, she left. He sat in his chair and basked in the power of darkness; he would become very familiar with it. In a small corner of his mind, he felt a prick of awareness but disregarded it. Finally, he was in control, this was going to be fun.

The memory settled again, like a murky film, into the back of his mind. He rubbed his bleary eyes and stared at his reflection in the mirror. As he contemplated himself, something caught his eye and he bent forward to examine it more closely. There was a dark rim around his blue eyes, as often as he had admired himself, he had never noticed it. He couldn't remember if it had always been there or not. What did it mean, if it hadn't? Before he could think about it anymore, a knock sounded at his door.

"Come in."

"Your Majesty, everyone is present and awaiting you in the throne room."

"Very well, I will be there shortly."

David glanced one last time at his reflection and what he saw made him smile. He was a man, clothed in the very best robes, powerful enough to have anything he wanted and he wanted everything. His mother had taught him well. He slammed the door behind him, destiny was calling.

Chapter 15

THE THRONE ROOM WAS CROWDED with dignitaries from every region. Some came out of respect, others out of curiosity, but everyone came to see the drastic change that had come over David. It had been well-known that he was a self-absorbed man-child who had shown no interest in ruling. So it came as a shock to everyone when they received the missive inviting them to his coronation.

Lord Vicrano stood by his daughter and her husband, across the aisle from Lord Alcherist and Lord Overton. The glares coming his way made him want to laugh. Khal was safely hidden away in his manor and would remain so as long as Lord Alcherist behaved in a manner that pleased him. He grinned, giving the men a slight nod and saw Overton grab his brother in a white-knuckle grip. They exchanged rapid whispers, and with a final loathsome glance from Alcherist, they moved to watch the proceedings from another part of the room.

Lady Devona stood by the throne, the crown she had worn only recently now rested on a pillow in her hands. She looked weaker than he remembered from their meeting, her eyes cast downward instead of surveying the room for her next alliance. Trumpets sounded as her son David was announced and strutted in, instantly the room erupted into a wave of murmurs. Was this the same man? It couldn't be! This man walked with confidence, he looked neither to the left nor to the right, his intense gaze was fixed on the throne as though it had always been his sole desire. Lord Vicrano narrowed his eyes, something was amiss. He watched Devona and saw her eyes widen. Even though she tried to hide it, the pillow held in her hand trembled slightly as David stopped before her. She was afraid!

He glanced around the room to see if anyone else had noticed the changes in Lady Devona and his eyes landed on a familiar face that he couldn't quite place. As his eyes lingered, the man must have felt his stare because he looked around for the source, finding it, his own eyes widened and he scurried away. *Interesting*, Vicrano thought. He paid little attention to the transfer of the crown. The advisors droned on and on and made David, now King David, swear all sorts of rubbish that he knew he would not see through. When it was finally over, they retired to the dining hall.

Vicrano pulled his daughter to the side to ask her opinion on the matter.

"Before you say anything Father, yes, I know something is not right here. That is not the same David to whom I was intended. This David is someone who should not be toyed with. There is darkness in him that is very familiar to me. Do we know who their main Oracle is? We should have a conversation with him or her."

Vicrano was always impressed with how his daughter's mind worked. Her idea of a conversation usually left someone dead or severely impaired.

"I saw a man earlier and felt he was familiar. There he is creeping about the edges of the crowd trying to keep his face hidden from me."

"I see him. Well, well, well, now this all makes sense Father," she said with a chuckle.

"That man is Chumbra. He was banished from Arcana for practicing questionable medicine. At least *he* called it medicine. He was really experimenting on individuals who were desperate to awaken their latent gifts. Most went mad and had to be put down. A few still roam the mountain side and are the basis of stories told to children to scare them into obedience. I suspect Devona asked him to help David and this is the result."

Vicrano turned to watch Devona seated two seats away from the king, the seats to his right and left were now occupied by men with ties to the dark lord. My how the mighty have fallen.

"We will see how this plays out, Daughter. I assume we still have our little birds in place?"

She nodded. "Good, very good. Come, let us eat and see where the tides take us."

Chapter 16

AKRONIUS WOKE TO THE WARMTH and soft light of the sun and the scent of fresh bread. He could not recall ever having eaten and slept so well as during these last few weeks spent with Wleia. He stretched his arms above his head and heard a soft growl.

"Aww cut the act mutt! We both know your bark is the only thing you have. You are as soft as the bread your mistress has prepared." He shook his head, "now I am talking to animals. I have been here too long."

Akronius walked outside to see the final shades of a pink sunrise turning to the brilliant blue of a new day. He had grown comfortable here. Without the watchful eyes of Queen Devona, his days had been peaceful. He did an honest day's work and went to bed sore and tired but with a new sense of accomplishment. He had heard the whispers from the manor about the coronation taking place, and perhaps he should have gone, but the thought of returning there... He looked down and dislodged a rock from the dirt with his toe and then kicked it further in frustration. He had learned nothing here other than that Wleia loved her twins and was a widow. Apparently, twins ran in her family, she herself was one. Her twin brother had died trying to save her husband from a flash flood, the bodies were never recovered. Akronius could recall that rainy season. There had been many flash floods and many lives lost. Wleia had simply nodded, and Akronius knew her faith in The One was strong. He had never given it much thought, just lived each day and did what was needed, but these last few weeks had made him question his purpose. Wleia hadn't spoken directly about her beliefs; she just lived it, quietly but strongly. She blessed every meal. She thanked The One for everything no matter how small. She *lived* gratefully and it shook him to the core. This life by the river was a direct contrast to the one he had been accustomed to at the manor. Since Devona had taken over, darkness had settled into the halls. He closed his eyes and inhaled deeply, without intending to he had come to love the sunshine.

"The One will bring another sunrise tomorrow, I promise. Come in for breakfast Akronius, there is fresh bread and plenty of eggs. Thanks to that new feed you showed me, the hens are laying as never before. Al will be so excited when he gets back. He loves eggs, well food in general really." She laughed as she walked inside with him trailing behind her.

He had learned much about her small family, none of which Devona would find useful. He did not know what he would do, but he would have to return soon.

"Food is better enjoyed when you eat it Akronius, not stare at it. What's the matter?" She had grown accustomed to his company and found he was not at all the evil man she initially thought him to be. He was misguided, misinformed and sadly, very confused about who he was meant to be. In the grand scheme of things, he had been a pawn, a blunt object used to hurt others. He took orders and carried them out and now he found himself rudderless. Wleia had tried to see past the marks on his face to the man beneath and she believed she had succeeded. She spoke of her children at every opportunity in the hopes that he would develop a deeper understanding of them and their love for each other. Hopefully, when the time came, for she knew eventually he would be faced with making a decision that would impact them all, she prayed he would base it on the time they had spent together and all she had shared with him.

"I have to return to the manor soon, to Devona. And I feel conflicted about it. I've never questioned my duties or my loyalties before now. I have always been a sharp object used to get a point across. But now I see there is something to be said and gained from a peaceful existence. I do not know how to reconcile the two parts of me with this new understanding." He toyed with his food, pushing it from one side to the other, mirroring the debate she knew was going on in his head and heart.

Wleia took a moment to collect her thoughts, and ask The One for wisdom in her response to the troubled man seated before her.

"We each have two sides to us Akronius, a light and a darkness that battle every day, in every decision we make, in every word and thought. Each day we must decide which will win, who we will be, and then stand by that decision no matter the cost. You have never had to make that decision consciously because no one ever asked you to. You were always told to choose the dark; you were trained for it, by it, in it. But light and dark do not coincide peacefully; one will always overpower the other. You must choose which."

He listened to her wisdom and soaked it up as he had over many meals these last few weeks. She stared at him as if there were more she wanted to say but couldn't, or wouldn't.

"I leave in the morning, Wleia. I will keep your words in mind."

The next morning was overcast and Akronius couldn't help but wonder how well it mirrored his thoughts. He stood in the doorway watching as Wleia packed a small meal for him to carry on his journey.

"Wleia, you know I came here searching for the heir to the throne. I thought you had hidden him somehow. I came seeking one thing and found something else entirely." He looked out into the forest where he would soon venture, "I will never forget your kindness and compassion."

"You are welcome. You can come back whenever you need a breath of fresh air... or some fishing!" She glanced down. He knew she was searching for the right way to say something. "One day you will face a great decision, Akronius. Remember this place when that time comes."

He looked at her and nodded. His sword was fastened around his waist and felt strangely foreign to him, after not wearing it for so long. He picked up the pack she had made for him and set off to see what his future held.

Chapter 17

THROUGH HER SPIES, DEVONA had learned Akronius was on his way back to the manor and left instructions that he be brought to her chambers immediately upon his return. She prayed to anyone listening that he had good news for her. In light of what was taking place now, she just might help the brat overthrow her son. She paced the length of her room deep in thought. "What is taking so long?" She stepped out into the hallway. "You there, where is the captain? He was to be brought to me immediately."

"Your Maj.... Umm, Lady Devona, Captain Akronius was brought to the throne room at King David's behest."

Devona was speechless. David showed absolutely no interest in any of this before the change. She had started a mental catalog of things before and after the change, he was so drastically different. It was as if he were an entirely different man. What did this mean? She would have to request an audience with him because he no longer allowed her free access, mother or not. Would he share the information or hide something? She was unaccustomed to being the one in the dark. She did not like it at all!

"King David, I trust you are finding your feet in this new role with ease?" Akronius said, as he looked around the room. There were no mirrors in sight and no Devona, though there were several new advisers present, dark lord affiliates by the look of them.

"Yes Akronius, I find it suits me rather well. Mother may not have the best methods, but the results have been wondrous. Now what news do you have of my long-lost cousin?"

"Your Majesty, I am afraid I found no trace of him or the woman."

"Is that so?"

Akronius grew uncomfortable under the stare of the king. There was a blackness in his eyes that was very unsettling and which had not been there before. He had seen this child grow up, but he had no idea who he was now.

"Well, we will have to expand our search then. It is common knowledge that every young person seeks out the wisdom of a great Oracle for training. I assume my cousin would do the same. Shama is the Oracle my aunt trusted the most and she would have sent him there for training had she lived. You will journey there and seek him out. Kill my cousin if you find him. Kill the Oracle whatever happens. Kill yourself if you fail in either of these missions, understood?" He issued these orders as if he were discussing the weather, entirely void of feeling.

Akronius's face paled, "Yes, Your Majesty."

"You may leave."

"Yes Sire."

"Akronius…"

He turned to the king.

"I'll know if you try to deceive me."

The smile that played across the king's face sent chills down every inch of Akronius's body. It was absolutely evil.

"Your Majesty, your mother requests an audience." A servant said from the open door.

"Of course she does. Send her in."

Akronius and Devona passed each other in the doorway. A sheen of sweat covered his face as their eyes met. Her breathing quickened, both could tell the power had shifted in the kingdom and neither was prepared for the all-consuming darkness of it.

"Mother, welcome, welcome! What can I do for you? Do you need another gown? Would you like the cook to prepare a *special* meal for you? Perhaps you need to take an indefinite trip somewhere?"

"Your humor is memorable as always Your Majesty. But no, I would never dream of leaving your side at such a time. Even a king needs his mother, and it would send a bad message to your *people* should I go missing. No, I am curious about the news brought by Akronius, about my nephew. Was he found?"

"Tsk, tsk, Lady Devona. You know women are excluded from matters of the state. Don't you worry your little head. I have it well in hand." King David watched his mother flounder for a reason to ask for the information again. He rather liked seeing her squirm. Having to ask him for anything was a new low point for an ambitious woman like her. He let her suffer a few moments more before answering her.

"But to assuage your curiosity, no he was not found. I have sent Akronius on to finish the task you were unable to do. He is heading to the same place my cousin would have gone, had his mother lived long enough to send him. I am surprised you did not think of it yourself mother. Mind you, I still doubt that he is alive at all, but in the event he is, *my* captain of the guard will dispatch him and Shama, the Oracle he would seek for training."

Devona's eyes widened in shock. Shama was the oldest living Oracle of The One. To harm him was considered sacrilege, inviting the wrath of The One on the whole country. Even she would not have gone to such lengths. The Oracles in their employ were pawns, little better than soothsayers, but *Shama.* They would be doomed.

"My King, there is a *reason* I did not follow that course of action! Do not pursue this, you know of his value to The One. It is said he has seen Him and *lived!* You cannot…"

"DO NOT tell me what I CANNOT do! I am your KING! You will obey me or you will DIE!" His whole body trembled with the force of the tirade and she took a step back. She would pay for this with her life. She knew that now. Her son was gone, and the kingdom would not be far behind him. It was as if she was seeing him for the first time, greed had clouded her vision but now the darkness surrounding her son, the king, was evident. A solitary tear slid down her cheek as she dipped into a low curtsy and turned to leave the room.

Chapter 18

SHE STOOD JUST OUTSIDE THE DOOR, listening to the low murmurs of the king and his advisers, wondering what she could do to correct the situation. Out of her line of sight, movement caught her eye and she turned to see Akronius beckon her. Apprehensively, she approached him.

"Yes?"

"Lady Devona, what happened to David?"

"I have no idea what you are talking about. David has simply grown into the man he was meant to be all along. I always knew he was strong, now everyone else can see it as well."

"Mistress, there is a darkness in these halls that was not here when I departed. I am all for the widening of our borders but this... something is wrong here."

She stared at him silently. She could admit her guilt to herself but never to anyone else. All that was left was her pride at this point. "Developed a conscience in recent days, have you? Yet you go on a mission to kill the most revered Oracle in the country. I am not surprised you recognize the darkness so easily, Akronius; you live and breathe it."

"People can change Devona, if they want to." He held eye contact as long as he could before turning and walking away. He was tempted to tell her that he had no intention of killing the Oracle, but he sensed no change in her. She would always be a self-absorbed, manipulative woman. She thought she was in control, one step ahead of everyone else. Little did she know none of them were really in control, someone was always pulling the strings or directing their steps. Whether toward the light or away from it was the only difference.

Devona watched him walk out of the manor and then rushed to Chumbra's chambers.

"Chumbra, prepare me a similar vial to what we gave David. I need to be able to face whatever is coming. Power is shifting like the seasons and I refuse to be blown away with the chaff."

"Of course, Mistress, I do not have the ingredients for the exact dose we gave the king but I can make one similar. Wait here." He walked off through a separate door, and she could hear him chanting to himself and mixing things.

She could only hope the dose she received would not possess as much darkness as David's seemed to.

"Mistress, here is yours. The same rules apply, take this just before you retire for the night and you will awaken your gifts by morning." Chumbra could barely contain his excitement. He had been banished from his home for dabbling in these experimental treatments, but no one needed to know that. When he heard they were seeking a new Oracle he simply made sure he was the one selected. He had created many monsters in the past, most he had managed to contain or kill, a few may have escaped to roam the mountains, but no one was any the wiser. He feared he would have been ousted at the coronation when Lord Vicrano spotted him, but he did not seem to recognize him, at least he hoped he hadn't. He was getting closer to the perfect combination; David was proof of that for he only displayed a few symptoms of mania. Chumbra used the exact opposite of every ingredient in this new version, save for the blood, he would see how Lady Devona fared in the morning.

Devona took the vial and looked at it in surprise. Where David's was thick, almost gelatinous, hers was fluid. Where his had been dark, hers was crystal clear. She placed it in her pocket and turned to go.

"Mistress, do let me know how it turns out for you." Devona gave the barest nod before exiting his room. "I will be most curious to see the changes." He added once she was out of ear shot.

She was having doubts about his sanity. He thought no one knew of his banishment, but she knew. She knew all about his poisoning the other Oracle who she had initially accepted. At the time she approved of his cunning and ambitions, now she was not so sure. Perhaps he truly was a madman. But for her he was a means to an end.

Chapter 19

AKRONIUS HEADED STRAIGHT FOR HIS quarters. Being captain of the guard, he was not required to bunk with his men. It had been over a month since he was there. He paused on the threshold and looked around. Everywhere he looked there were trophies of his life's work. Swords taken from vanquished enemies, the spoils of secret missions, jewelry, weaponry and other useless trinkets, but his most prized possession was in his room. He walked and stood before the cage. In it was a rare bird. He had hired a man to care for it in his absence, and was glad it fared well. The bird was supposed to have the most beautiful song, as well as the deadliest poison in its talons, but he had never heard it sing, and he had its talons clipped periodically. It never sang for him, only watched him with intelligence and sometimes loathing. As he stood before it, he was overcome with a terrible sense of guilt. And, as if sensing this, the bird tilted its head and chirped once, something it had never done in the past. Before he knew what was happening, Akronius found himself pouring out his soul to this bird. He confessed every heinous act, every murderous plot and treacherous deed. He laid bare everything he could remember and sighed as a sense of peace settled over him. He didn't realize his list of sins was so long. He had knelt before the cage all night and it was now sunrise. He looked up into the bird's eyes and knew he had to release it. He carried the tiny aviary outside into the dawn.

"I am sorry my friend for holding you in captivity, keeping you away from the sun and wind. I thought to keep your beauty to myself and that is wrong. I hope you won't hold a grudge against me. Maybe one day I will be fortunate enough to hear your song." He took a deep breath and opened the delicate gilded door, but the bird made no rush at freedom. It simply cocked its head and chirped again. "Alright then, if you decide to kill me it would be well deserved, but I hope you won't and we can part on better terms than we lived."

Akronius extended his arm into the cage, the bird looked at it and then at him. Slowly, it lifted one taloned claw. Never breaking eye contact, it gently placed it around Akronius' wrist and then it lifted the other. Akronius exhaled and withdrew his arm with the bird from the cage. He stood there admiring the way the sun moved over the feathers, he had never seen the colors look so vibrant. A light breeze blew through the trees and the bird blinked as if it had just realized where it was. Akronius could feel it gather itself and then launch into the air with one stroke of its glorious wings.

It shot straight into the path of the sun and seemed to linger there as if absorbing the sun's rays, its shadow covered Akronius as he stood below. Its feathers glinted and refracted the light like jewels, and then it dived back toward him. Akronius held his ground, he may have been repentant but he would not go down without a fight. The bird pulled up at the last moment and hovered above his head. Then it opened its beak and the most beautiful yet haunting sound came out. The bird's song was indescribable and it soothed him like a balm on an open wound. He couldn't help but close his eyes and let the trills and chirps surround him as they echoed in the early morning silence. When he opened his eyes, the bird was gone and a single ruby and jade colored feather floated toward him. He caught it and tucked it inside his vest. His soul had been cleansed and now he had to clean his home. He decided to sell the spoils he had collected and donate the proceeds to families he knew were in need. He gave a large portion to his household servants along with an apology; he had not accepted their loyalty with gratitude.

Wleia sat and watched the sunset over the mountains and offered another prayer of protection for her children. Naia rested her head against her knee and whined. Wleia stroked her soft fur and whispered, "It's alright Naia, The One will provide and protect as He always has. We need only trust and obey when necessary." She braced herself on the stick she now depended on to walk and stand.

After suffering from a fall a few days ago, she was in constant pain. Her body did not heal as quickly as it once had, and her stores of dried meat and fruits were dangerously low. She did not have the strength to forage. She relied on the rain to collect water since she could not carry the bucket to the river and it had been several days since the last downpour. Naia had occasionally brought home a fresh rabbit or pheasant, but she was still young and not the best huntress. Soon they would be out of food and water. Still, she trusted. Somehow things would turn out the way they were meant to, on this side of life or on the other.

She slowly limped her way to her room and sank onto the bed. With a sigh, she tucked herself beneath the pelt of the mother wolf and drifted off to sleep.

Naia sat and watched her for several hours before slipping silently into the night. She was not a pet and therefore the door was never locked. Wleia had taught her how to open it herself and left a rope on the outside to pull it shut behind her. Something was wrong, Naia could smell it on the woman. Death was coming for her. Naia sat and howled her grief to the moon. As her voice trailed off, she felt an urge to run. She allowed herself to be led by the unusual tug and ran through the night. She did not slow when she crossed paths with a herd of deer, nor did she shy from the farmer who threw stones at her. She did not stop for food, water or to rest, something kept pushing her. She panted and foamed from the pace she set but could not, would not stop. As dawn approached, she found herself on the outskirts of a town. She sniffed until she caught a familiar scent. Yes, this was right. She followed her nose to the door of a small house and scratched. No one stirred, so she settled in to rest, finally.

Chapter 20

AKRONIUS STIRRED FROM WHAT HAD been the best sleep since his time by the river. His soul felt refreshed as he inhaled deeply. He got up to start his morning meal. He opened the door to gather wood for a fire, and tripped over something across his threshold.

"What in the world are you doing here?" Naia looked at him the same as she always had, like he was an imbecile. "Where is Wleia?" He looked around and did not find her. Upon closer inspection he could see the pup's feet left bloody prints where she stood and her coat was matted. "Come inside Pup, you look as if you've traveled all this way for a reason. Let's get you cleaned up and fed."

She obediently followed him inside and let him minister to her wounds. After they both ate, she went to the door and whined.

"Alright," Akronius said, "go about your business then."

Naia went out and returned quickly. She yipped at him and then went out again. She repeated this three times before Akronius figured out that she wanted him to follow her. But, when he did, she growled and went back inside. When she came out with his empty pack, Akronius let loose a loud bark of laughter. It had been a long time since he felt this lightness that enabled him to laugh.

"Oh, so we are going on a trip then?" Akronius sobered quickly. He did have a journey he was supposed to be taking. He supposed he could make a detour, and decide his next steps along the way. Wleia's wisdom would be a great help in that regard.

"Alright then, let's pack."

He took the bag and went back into the house. He glanced around and wondered what to bring. This time he had no intention of killing anyone, still he may need his sword for protection. He looked at it with disgust. The blood of so many innocents stained its blade. He couldn't bring himself to carry it. He would have to buy a new one along the way. He gathered his belongings and was ready to set out by midday.

"Alright Pup, lead the way." Naia barked her agreement and set off at a brisk pace with Akronius on her heels.

As night fell on Elhaanai, Lady Devona retired to her room. She took out the vial and placed it on her table. She sat and stared at it, contemplating her next actions. There would be no going back, she may be changed into the most powerful woman or she may descend into the mania she was starting to notice in King David. He was often seen walking through the halls muttering to himself, the staff had started giving him a wide berth when he passed. No one knew when his patience would snap and he would lash out at whoever happened to be nearest. Their prison cells were overflowing thanks to King David and his short temper. Devona picked up the vial and watched the firelight flicker through its clear center. Opening it, she tipped its contents into her mouth and stared into the flames as she swallowed.

Slowly, a tingle began in her toes and made its way up her legs to her torso, spreading outward to her arms and her head. She felt like a million ants were crawling all over her. She started scratching and couldn't stop, not even when her skin started peeling away under her fingertips. Shedding like a snake! A moan started low in her belly and forced its way out. She fell to the floor and writhed in agony. The pain was immeasurable, and then it got worse. Heat was pouring from every part of her body. She felt as if she were being cooked from the inside out. She crawled to the bedside table for the pitcher of water left there by her handmaid. Her body was no longer her own and jerked about uncontrollably from the pain, causing her to knock the pitcher over into her face. Instead of providing a cool reprieve from the heat, the liquid evaporated on contact with her skin. She was boiling within her own skin. All she could do was curl in on herself and wait for it all to end.

Chapter 21

INHALE, EXHALE. She could feel her chest expand with each breath, so she was still alive. She sat up and evaluated how she felt. She lay naked before the fire. The ash surrounding her must be the remnants of her clothing. Her door cracked open and she rushed to cover herself.

"Mistress? Are you alright? We heard you crying out through the night. Are you well?" Her handmaiden looked around the room quickly and then entered. "I wonder where she has gone so early. The wretched woman never leaves without berating me at least once. And look at all this ash! Tsk, tsk, heaven forbid she actually cleans up after herself. What did she do, build a fire in the middle of the room? Imagine a grown woman being so messy. And what is this... skin? Oh, heaven help us, she has returned to dabbling in the dark arts."

Devona's mouth dropped in shock. "How *dare* you speak so callously of me? Who do you think you are? I'll have you flogged for your insolence!"

"Ahh my Mistress," the maid whipped around, her eyes searching the room. "Mistress, where are you?" Her trembling hands dropped the skin.

"Your stupidity truly has no bounds!"

"Oh, my Mistress, I don't know what kind of darkness you have aligned yourself with, but I want no part of it! First, the king and now you! One, protect us all!" The woman glanced around once again and fled the room.

Devona stood in shock and then started laughing. "She couldn't see me. This is perfect!"

Devona twirled in excitement and then stopped. "Now how do I turn it off?" She started to quickly dress and then stopped. She would be cold, but she did not know if her ability had transferred to her clothing, since what she had on last night, burned. She had to assume that it didn't. Naked, she hurried toward the Oracle's chamber. On her way she was able to listen in on a myriad of conversations that otherwise would have halted instantly at her approach.

The general feel of the manor was fear, all the staff lived in constant fear of King David. They worried about their sons being sent off to join the army, they worried he would require their daughters to attend to him at his whim. They whispered of the good Queen Alanna, and how they missed the days of peace and certainty. She scowled to herself. She would be a better queen than Alanna, and she would *certainly* be a better ruler than her mad son. She just had to play the game right.

She entered the Oracle's room silently and watched as he looked up in confusion.

"Who is there?"

"Your Queen."

"My... what? Devona?" Chumbra backed up until he bumped into a chair and sat.

"Yes Chumbra, your concoction had an interesting effect as you can see or rather *not* see." He could hear the smile in her voice, though he had no idea where she stood. He could feel his pulse quickening as his eyes darted around the room. He felt her fingertips brush the back of his neck and he toppled from his chair with surprise. Devona cackled with delight at his response.

"You're invisible! How remarkable!"

"Yes, yes, it is. Now, how do I become visible again?"

"Let me think for a moment. This gift hasn't been seen in decades. Let me get my books." He scurried about looking for his notebooks. "Did you shed your skin?"

"Yes, quite painfully I might add. I don't know how snakes do it so frequently." She muttered off to his right. Though he had been staring straight ahead, he got the feeling she kept moving to toy with him.

"Yes, the skin, you need to keep the skin with you to revert back. You would have experienced burning and itching as you shed. That feeling will lessen as you master your gift."

"But what do I *do* with the skin Chumbra? Rub myself with it?

Slip back into it? Burn it? Eat it?"

He could hear the frustration in her voice. "Yes, Mistress.
You, umm, you have to eat it. You could cook it or steep it for tea."
He glanced anxiously around. He didn't like this at all.

"I see." She whispered directly into his ear. He swallowed
audibly.

"You must keep the skin with you at all times. If anyone else
were to get it and eat it, you would be invisible until that person died.
Then you would have to burn their body, and eat the ashes to be
visible again. Mistress? Lady Devona, are you still here?" His voice
quivered while Devona sat directly across from him and smiled.

It was amazing the level of fear one could inspire by simply
being unseen. She watched him walk about his room doing small
tasks, constantly glancing around the room and over his shoulder,
conducting meetings with other household staff members for
solutions to various ailments, and when she was sure his guard was
down, she approached him. He was busy cutting herbs and placing
them in jars. She reached forward and lifted the knife,

"Aaarrrggghhh!" He choked on his fear.

"I know all about your banishment Chumbra, and I'll be
watching you. Always." She whispered as she nicked his cheek just
below his eye and let the knife fall with a clatter. She stayed long
enough to watch him slump over the table and hear a small sob
escape. She smiled and gently closed the door behind her.

When she got back to her room, the skin still lay by her bedside
table. She picked it up and placed a small piece in her mouth. It
melted away and tasted like the sweetest candy she ever had. She
closed her eyes in delight. She quickly ate the rest of it and felt
tingles begin in her toes. She sat in preparation for the burning and
when it came, it was not as intense as the first time, closer to a
severely high fever. After a while, everything subsided and she
dressed again. Leaving her chambers, she headed to the throne
room, but guards stopped her before she could enter.

"M'Lady, the King is still meeting with advisors and has given
strict orders that no one is to disturb him. Not even you."

Devona answered demurely, "I understand. Thank you." With
a smile she headed back to her room. She would practice over and

over until she mastered this gift. Then she could start planning for her rise to power once again.

Chapter 22

KING DAVID GLANCED AROUND at his advisors. They were the wealthiest in his region and therefore held the most sway in matters of state. To those without gifts, money equated to power. They were fat and lazy and did whatever he said, as long as the food and wine flowed freely. He slumped on his throne and rubbed his temples as one of them droned on about poor crops and an increase in strange vagrants.

"What is your name again? Actually, it doesn't matter." He waved the man away before he could answer. "I don't care about crops or your homeless vagabonds. Where do we stand with the alliances? Has work begun on the pass to… has it begun?" His memory was getting worse each day.

"Yes, Your Majesty. We are felling trees and Lord Vicrano has sent some of his men to help. It will still be quite some time before the road is clear enough for travel."

"Very well. Leave me now."

The men walked out slowly, no one said a word. They had quickly learned the king's hearing was questionable. If he even thought you said something contrary, he would have you arrested and thrown in jail. Silence was the best way to guarantee one's survival.

King David waited until everyone had left before getting up. He moved to the wall and looked around once more. He always felt eyes watching him and had taken extra precautions to guard his own life. He pressed the wall sconce and it slid away revealing a dark hallway. These secret passageways were all over his manor. No one knew of them, he was safe. No, that wasn't true. His mother knew of them. He hadn't seen her in several days. He should pay her a visit. He altered his course for her room. No, he shouldn't be in the passageway, because then she would know about them. He emerged in the hallway not far from her room. As he stepped out of the shadows, he bumped into a servant girl carrying a tray. It clattered to the floor and he bent to retrieve it. In doing so, he saw his reflection. His eyes had sunken into his head and his hair lay like sweat soaked strings; and then, it smiled at him and began to laugh!

"No! No mirrors! Guards arrest this girl at once for her dark arts and disobedience!"

The guards rushed to his aid but saw no one. There was a suit of armor, and a shield lying on the floor by the King's feet.

The guards looked around in confusion, "Your Majesty?"

"Arrest her you fools!"

"Yes Sir!" They picked up the shield and made a show of speaking for his benefit.

"Come on Girl, you know where you are heading."

They placed the shield behind the curtain and walked away. Looking at the king with skepticism.

Down the hall, Lady Devona silently watched everything. Her son was a handsome man, not a hair out of place, but he had lost his mind. What he saw when he looked in mirrors she did not know, but whatever it was he feared it. He did not practice his gift, each time he had, he would change a little more. He was anxious and paranoid. He decreed mirrors and all reflective items illegal and had them stripped from the walls or covered. Trays were now made of wood and all their polished silver and gold was locked away. He refused to tell anyone the reasons for his strange behavior.

Lady Devona went back inside and locked her door. Then she removed all her clothing, sat in front of the hearth and began her mantra. She hummed while she focused on the flames before her. When the first tingling in her toes began, she closed her eyes and imagined a flame in her belly that spread in all directions. Once she was consumed with the heat, she started peeling the skin from her forehead down. Once she got to her neck, she stood and removed it like a dress, stepping out of it. She had almost mastered the skill. It was no longer painful but still took entirely too much time; she would have to find a faster way. She folded the skin, placed it in a jewelry box and locked it. She unlocked her door and exited.

She turned the corner and almost collided with King David. He was standing in the shadows not moving but whispering to himself.

"Where was I going? To see someone? Mother. Yes, I was going to see my mother. But why? She doesn't love you. She manipulated you for her own ends. She wants the crown. She will kill you." He shook his head to clear it and looked up in a daze. "What? No. No, I'll go see mother, she will explain everything. She will tell me what to do." But he still headed in the opposite direction and Devona trailed quietly behind him.

She watched as the servants scurried out of his way even though he acknowledged no one. She listened as he continued to speak to himself as if to another person. Devona understood he was quite mad now. Something had taken hold of his mind when he swallowed the potion. She feared the same would happen to her. She stopped trailing him. There was only one way to find out, she turned and headed for Chumbra.

Chapter 23

DEVONA WAITED OUTSIDE CHUMBRA'S closed door until someone came to see him and she could slip inside unnoticed. Chumbra had become quite paranoid since her last visit. He glanced about nervously and constantly moved around the room waving his arms, never staying in one place too long. It was actually hilarious to watch his antics. He exhausted himself daily.

Devona made her way to a corner and settled in to wait. She needed to know where he kept his books on gifts. She had research to do.

Finally, Chumbra left the room for a meal. He locked the door behind him which did not bother her at all. She started opening every cupboard and drawer with no success. She racked her brain to remember where he had gone the last time she was here. She looked around, walked to a hutch, set into the wall and started feeling for secret panels. Finally, there was a shift on the very last shelf, a false bottom. There lay all his notes. She quickly leafed through them until she came to the one about her gift. She already knew most of what was written, but there were several tidbits he had kept to himself. There was a way to shift with clothing, it was harder to learn and the clothing had to be specially made. Walking about naked was alright since no one could see her, but she did get cold. Also, it was the only gift where madness was not listed as a possible side effect. She flipped the pages until she found one titled shadow walker, which is what she assumed her son had developed into. The ingredients for a reversal antidote would be hard to come by. She would have to start work on it immediately. She tore the page out and placed the book back where she found it.

She didn't have to wait long for Chumbra to return. He entered quickly and slammed the door behind him. She did not have time to exit, *no matter*, she thought, *time to play a little*. As he moved further into the room, Lady Devona threw open the door and let loose a banshee wail. Chumbra dropped to the floor in a dead faint and Devona walked down the halls laughing out loud, sending everyone in every direction with fear.

Once she had returned to her physical form, she summoned her personal servant.

"I need you to gather these items for me as quickly and discreetly as possible."

The list read...

4 drops of blood from the Hydnellum Peckii
1 bloom of toxicoscordion venenosum
1 vine of cuscuta
10 stingers from the gympie tree
2 pods from the actaea pachypoda
Nectar from 1 corpse flower
1 vial of sap from the dracaena tree

"Some of these will be quite difficult and costly to acquire."

"You already have access to the stores of treasure locked away, take what you need and be gone. Return with every item no matter the cost."

"As you wish." He bowed and left, heading toward the treasury. Lady Devona need not know he had suppliers everywhere, it would not be as difficult to get these items and not nearly as costly as he implied, but it helped to line one's pockets for incidentals. Besides, if there was a slight discrepancy in what he collected or spent, she would never know. He would return in a week, that would be enough time to give the semblance of having worked hard for the items.

It was in the early morning hours when Akronius reached the riverside house. Naia made a beeline for the front door and scratched with no response. Akronius walked slowly behind her and opened the door. He knew that smell, it was sickness and death. He rushed to Wleia's bedroom door and stopped short. She was lying very still and he feared he was too late. He rubbed Naia on her head.

"Good girl" he said, receiving a heartbreaking whimper in response.

He approached the bedside and exhaled deeply as he saw her chest rise and fall, though sluggishly.

"Wleia, that mongrel you adopted ran all the way to the city to fetch me here. You are obligated to wake up and thank her."

A small crack of her lips was the only sign he received that she had heard him.

"Alright then, my turn to take care of you it would seem."

Akronius went to the kitchen area and saw how poorly stocked she was. They were literally dying of starvation and lack of water. He took the bucket and raced to the river. It would be freezing but it was better than dehydration. He came back and immediately brought her a cup. She was too weak to sit up so he held her and let her take small sips.

"Thank you, Akronius. You have come to be like a son to me." Her whispered words came through lips that hardly parted, such was her weakness. She closed her eyes and rested against him.

"I never knew my mother. You are better than nothing." He had hoped she would laugh, but she was asleep again. He kissed her forehead because he knew she was not aware of it. Akronius was not one prone to displays of affection or emotions, but she truly had been a mother to his soul. He would bring her back to health, and leave her well stocked before starting his journey of discovery into the unknown.

Chapter 24

HE FASHIONED A SUNDIAL in her yard to mark the time. Every quarter hour he brought her more water. He did this until she had successfully drunk two cups. Then he gathered wood and made a fire. He surveyed her garden. She had been so meticulous about it when he was here. Now it lay fallow. He found a solitary potato and some strangled looking carrots. It would be a meager broth, but he wanted to start her off lightly. Just then the wolf pup came loping out of the woods, in her mouth was a pheasant. Akronius whooped with joy.

"You wonderful wolf you! Your mistress will be well before you know it." Akronius cleaned the bird and added a small portion of it to the broth. He also gave a large piece to Naia.

"Ok Mother, let's get you fed." Akronius helped her sit and spoon fed her the broth. She managed to eat half before falling asleep again. This was their routine for three days. Each day Naia brought a pheasant, and each day Akronius fed Wleia broth. On the fourth day, when he went to wake her, he found her already sitting up in bed.

"Well, my adopted son, today I would like eggs please." They both smiled because she was clearly on the mend.

"I would gladly provide those eggs, but we have no chickens."

Wleia chuckled, "look a little harder. Things aren't always what they seem."

He went back to the chicken coop that had appeared completely empty when he checked it last, only to see two beady eyes staring at him from under the hay! It had hidden from him, the cheeky so-and-so!

He reached to gather a few eggs and managed to get only one and several pecks for his trouble.

"This hen should be enlisted into his majesty's army. That is the sharpest beak I have ever encountered."

He cooked the egg as best he could, adding a bit of salt to it. It wasn't the best, but it wasn't the worst either.

"I'll be glad when you can get up and about, so you can keep house properly again. I am no cook."

Wleia looked at him and then as calmly as possible she told him, "I will not be leaving this bed, ever again, my dear."

"Come now, you are no crippled old woman! You have many good years yet. And your children will return. You will want to hear all about your family in the south."

"Akronius, look." She pulled the pelt away from her body and showed him her leg. She must have broken something when she fell and it healed poorly. Her leg was a ghastly shade of purple and black, dark veins made their way up and under her clothing. His jaw dropped and he noticed a slight sheen on her face from fever. How had he not noticed?

"No, Wleia!"

"Darling, we are past that. Just call me Mother, you have been a son to me as I said already. I did my best for you, and you have returned the favor. Let us enjoy this time together. Was Naia the only reason you came back? I am sure you missed me."

He knew she was changing the subject on purpose, he sighed deeply.

"You are right. I did miss you, but I had intended to travel this way in a week's time anyway. The king has ordered me to continue my search for Alanna's child. I am to kill him, and the Oracle he might seek, Shama."

At this, her face paled so much he feared she would keel over.

"What is it? Are you alright? Breathe Mother! Breathe!"

She took a deep shuddering breath and seemed to age right before his eyes. A single tear fell that was followed by another and then they were pouring down her cheeks. She clutched her fist to her mouth and sobbed into it.

"Please, tell me what troubles you! Perhaps I can help."

"Akronius, please. Stop. I need time. I will tell you... in time. Let me rest now."

He rose slowly and watched her turn her back on him. He

would give her what she asked for, though they didn't have much of it left.

The next day she refused to eat, he spent his time clearing her garden of dead plants and debris. He stocked the wood pile and went hunting, he actually managed to bring down a deer. It felt right, this living naturally, no gifts, no manipulation. Just living. As he skinned the deer, he heard Wleia call his name.

"Yes Mother?"

"Sit Akronius. We have much to speak about. First, I have some questions for you. Answer truthfully, no matter the result. Yes?"

"Yes."

"What has changed in the weeks since you left me? You are different and I want to know how and why."

"Where do I begin? I left you and went directly to see King David." He told her of the changes in the man, now King, and how Devona was afraid. He told her how his skin crawled when he spoke to the king; the darkness that he never noticed before seemed to permeate everything in the manor. Then he told her of his orders and how even Devona was against it. He felt the tears well up in his eyes as he recounted his night of cleansing and the release of the song bird. He showed her its feather, still soft and brilliant in color.

"Then I tripped over your pup and here we are."

"My, that is quite the tale. So much, in so little time will affect everything we do going forward. Thank you for your honesty, now it is my turn. She closed her eyes and took a deep breath. "I was born gifted as a scribe, not an uncommon gift, but one not very highly esteemed. I was also married as you know and lost my husband and brother to the flash floods while I carried our twins."

All this he knew, but he felt her gaze harden on him and understood something was about to change in their relationship with what she said next.

Chapter 25

"AKRONIUS, I KNOW WHO YOU ARE. Hear me, I know *who* you are. I always have." She closed her eyes and breathed deeply. When she found his gaze again, hers had turned to steel with determination.

"I found her in my barn, I scribed her message and I bore her son when the twin in my own womb perished." She paused to let him process this, his heart rate picked up, he stood and turned his back on her. She hadn't exactly lied to him, but she hadn't been forthright either. He paced as he tried to see it from her perspective. In all regards the heir was her son, she bore him, raised him and would naturally want to protect him. He turned back to see her looking at him with trepidation, she had risked everything to tell him this truth. He must prove himself worthy.

"Alright."

She smiled and continued with a conversation that would take them long into the night. He lit a candle and it burned until it went out, then he lit another before they had shared everything that needed to be said. She fell asleep, and he walked out into the dawn.

He was not a praying man, but after all he had learned and experienced it was hard to hold to his disbelief. He walked down to the river and sat on the chair facing the mountain.

"Okay, what should I call you, hmm? The One, as she does? A greater power? Whatever you are called, whoever you are, I hope you will listen to me. I am not someone who has lived well, but I am changing. Mostly, thanks to the woman you see laying there on her deathbed. She thinks this is her end, but if you are as powerful as she believes couldn't you heal her? Her children will need her, and I will need her guidance and wisdom. Would you really give her to me, have her change my life so drastically, only to take her from me at such a pivotal moment?" He stopped as if waiting for an audible answer but heard nothing. "Alright, so you'll take her from me and

77

then what am I supposed to do? You know of my orders. I am to kill *your* Oracle. Will you stand by and let that happen as well?” Akronius was growing angry in his frustration. Just when he was about to shout curses to the sky, he felt a hand on his arm. He whirled around and there stood Wleia.

“You are well! I prayed just this moment for this. He heard me. The One is real and actually heard me!” He went to wrap her in his arms, but she stepped back and smiled.

“Yes Akronius, The One is real and does listen to our prayers, even the ones spoken in anger and frustration. But He does not always answer in the way we expect or would like. You must promise me something now.”

“Anything, Mother. Anything at all.”

“Follow your orders.”

“What? You can’t possibly…”

She interrupted him with a raised hand and the smile he had grown accustomed to, the one that said she knew something he did not.

“Follow your orders and find my children, find the Oracle, and *protect* them. Care for them as you have for me. They will not trust you. Alric knows who you are, and though he may appear amicable, there will be fire brewing beneath the surface. Do not fight as you have been trained. Use your mind. Use your heart. But most of all, be strong and courageous, son of my heart, your future will be... difficult.”

“Of course, I expect to be hunted before long. Once the king learns of my defection, nowhere will be safe, but I will do this for you and for The One.”

“Thank you. Look, the sun rises. Let us enjoy it together.”

They turned as they had so often in the past and watched the sun break over the mountain peaks. It seemed extra bright this morning, the colors vibrant in a spectacular display. He turned to comment on it and found he was alone. Thinking she had gone back to the house he slowly walked back. He reached the door and a howl tore through the peacefulness of the morning. He threw open the bedroom door and found her lying as she had not so long ago.

His cry joined with Naia’s mourning. “Noooooo!” He fell to his knees and clasped her hand to his cheek. It was still warm. He lifted his tear-filled eyes to her face; she had the same small smile there. He realized she had met the dawn with him before making her final journey. The One had answered his prayer, not the way he wanted, but an answer nonetheless. He knew what his next steps would be. But first, he would honor her with a proper burial.

Akronius walked outside to survey her land for the perfect spot. His eyes slid past the garden she loved, to the chair she always sat in to watch the sunrise. Naia was already there, curled up with her nose under her tail. Winter was almost upon them. He could feel the chill coming. Soon the ground would be too hard to break. He grabbed a shovel and walked over to Naia.

"Good job Girl. She loved this spot. It is only fitting that she rests here as well."

He moved the chair aside and started to dig. She was a small woman so he didn't have much work to do. Then he set about gathering river stones. After he was finished, he took a dip in the river to wash the dirt and tears away. The freezing water stole his breath and wrapped him in silence as he submerged himself and allowed his grief to flow. Emerging trembling and weak he stumbled toward the empty house to dress in his best clothes and to gather Wleia. He wrapped her in the pelt she had made herself and carried her to the river. He laid her down there, covering her with earth and rock.

"You loved this spot, Mother. Though I am sure you have a much better view from where you are now. I will miss you. More than I have missed anyone in my whole life. We did not spend a lifetime together, but you have changed my life eternally and I am grateful. Be at peace, I will keep my promise to you. Come on Girl, we have work to do." Naia looked at him forlorn, but did not move from the graveside.

"I would stay here as well if I could, you take all the time you need. You know how to find me when you are ready."

Akronius went back into the house and gathered his belongings. He could not bear the thought of sleeping there one more night without her. Though her presence lingered, it was not the same. He prepared the small home for winter. He even set the contrary hen free. He had no doubt it would manage to survive until he returned or someone else laid claim to the property. As he looked around once more, his eyes fell onto a cloth-wrapped item in the corner. He lifted it and instantly knew it was a sword. He remembered asking Wleia about it once. She had said it belonged to her husband and had been passed down from generation to generation, son to son. Since Alric had no need of it, Wleia had said he could take it if he desired. He had refused because of course he had his own, but now....

He unwrapped the cloth to find a magnificent piece of workmanship. It shone as if it had been freshly oiled. The grip was etched with a curious swirling gold pattern but settled into his palm comfortably and the balance was perfect. He gave it a few turns before settling it back into its sheath and placing it on his back. He was ready.

He walked outside and latched the door behind him. Naia still lay by the grave. He whistled once and saw her ears turn in his direction, but she did not rise. He knew she would find him eventually as she had before. He turned to face the mountains.

"Ok then," he said, taking a deep breath. "One, protect and guide me please." He took one step and tripped over something at his feet, then got a wet tongue across his cheek and he couldn't help but laugh. "I knew you liked me Naia. Let's go." Together they started off toward the mountain.

Chapter 26

SACHEM, LADY DEVONA'S SERVANT, made his way to her chamber and knocked.

"Enter!"

"Mistress, I have everything you requested." He laid a satchel on the table.

"Well done. You may leave."

"Mistress, I am sure you understand these were not easy to come by. I went to great lengths for several items."

Devona knew he was angling for additional payment and smiled. "Of course, you did. Just as I am sure the extra funds you removed from the treasury will more than cover the unexpected expenses you incurred." She saw him pale slightly.

"Of course, Mistress. I'll just see myself out."

Devona waved him away and opened the pack to examine its contents. Everything seemed to be accounted for and in the correct quantities. She took out her bowl and pestle to begin mixing the ingredients.

Once she had finished a small pile of what looked like dough lay in the bowl. She fashioned it into a small cake and placed it into a small iron pot that was hanging over the hearth. She was no cook but she could still make a small cake. Once it was cooked, she left it to cool. She would place it with the king's meal that night. He had become so paranoid of others that he had started taking his meals in his room. She would bring it to him and offer an apology. It would appeal to his ego if she came humbly of her own accord. She hoped by morning he would be his old insipid self.

That night she had the cook prepare David's favorite meal and carried the tray to his room herself. She knocked,

"Come!"

His back was to the door when she entered, even with his new power, he was still unaware of danger.

"You took long enough, I am famished! If it happens again you will learn," he turned, mid-tirade and finally saw her. "Oh, Mother what are you doing here?" He eyed the food suspiciously.

"My King, I wanted to offer my apology for disrespecting your authority in the matter of your plan for Shama and the boy." Devona lowered herself into a deep curtsy. "I was wrong to doubt you and I offer my services in whatever way you see fit."

"Well, well, this is an interesting turn of events isn't it? And all my favorite foods, too? Prepared by your own hand? Like uncle's breakfast I presume?" He had a wicked glint in his eye. "I have an idea, let's eat together. If you are truly repentant, prove it."

"Of course, Your Majesty." Devona knew he would do this. She had hidden the cake under the other pastries on his platter. She broke a piece off each item with him watching like a hawk, the last cake she broke and palmed the piece but chewed like she had placed it in her mouth. They waited a few moments in silence, his eyes locked on her for any adverse reactions, her eyes downcast in submission.

"You surprise me, Mother. Perhaps you have a heart after all. You may go. I will inform you should I have need of your services." He dismissed her and bent over the plate, shoveling the food in like a child. As she closed the door, she saw him take a bite from the cake she had prepared. For the second time, she abandoned him to fate.

They stood at the mouth of the river and looked up at the majestic peaks of the mountain range and the waterfall tumbling down before them.

"Okay, where is this marker then?" Elainea said wearily.

The journey had been hard and tiresome. They had practiced their gifts every step of the way until they were almost second nature. Alric closed his eyes and used his second sight to inspect the area around them. There was a space just behind the waterfall that seemed to pulse with energy.

"Elainea, I may have found it, but it would be wise for you to search with your gifts and see what you find as well."

Elainea knelt and placed her hands on the soil, her eyes took on a green hue as she communed with the local flora. "There is a space behind the falls that is almost glowing with energy. There is also a small path that leads to it."

"Good, I saw the same thing. Let's go."

They headed toward the path that skirted just behind the falls. They were soon soaked and once they had passed through into a cave behind the falls, Alric stepped closer to Elainea in preparation for what came next. She closed her eyes to focus, the air all around them became super-heated and they were dry almost instantly.

"Well done! You didn't singe anything that time."

She couldn't help but laugh, he was right after all. Their clothes bore the burn marks of previous failed attempts. "I promise, your hair will grow back Brother."

He reached up in shock, praying she was joking. "You minx!" They laughed together. Laughter had kept them strong throughout the many lonely nights of missing home and their mother.

They turned simultaneously to search for the marker. Etched into the wall they found their next directions. The image depicted a compass pointing north and a stone outcropping in the shape of a crown. There was no distance, only a direction and destination.

"This makes no sense. North would be directly through the mountain." Elainea looked around, "we are surrounded by solid stone."

"Are we though? Look at the pool of water at the mouth of the cave. See how it ripples? There must be an opening somewhere."

Elainea hadn't noticed that; Alric was good with details like that. Probably a side effect of his gift of sight. They began on opposite sides of the cave feeling the walls as they moved toward the center, and then they both fell through.

"Amazing!" Alric exclaimed, "an illusion!"

Chapter 27

THEY STOOD AND SURVEYED the mountains surrounding them. There were several paths they could take, but how would they know the correct one? They could get lost and never find their way out.

Alric's eyes clouded over as he used his sight. There were four paths to choose from. The one to his left showed several skeletons impaled on spikes not far down the way. The one next to it showed nothing as did the other two. He levitated a rock and tossed it down the second path. Faster than he could believe possible, something shot from the wall and snatched the rock. It looked like a web of some kind. He could hear the crunching of teeth and knew that was not the path to take. No wonder there were no bones. He shuddered.

"Elainea, are you seeing this as well?"

"Yes. I never did like spiders or whatever that was. And those spikes are well hidden. These last two both look promising, although one is so dark, I can barely see more than a short distance and the other is weirdly silent."

"All of them head north. We will have to take a chance."

"Or we could try to join our gifts again."

"Alric, the last time we tried that I ended up being thrown nearly a mile, and you had your fingertips singed. We are not ready."

"One more time, Elainea. The Oracle will test us and we need to be as prepared as possible to shorten our training time."

She sighed deeply and extended her hand. It was as if a current passed from one to the other on contact, they both inhaled sharply. Alric tried his sight again and could see that the third path ended in a dead end, so that left the dark path. He let go of his sister's hand and bent at the waist breathing deeply.

"Wow. If we can learn to control that, we would be almost unstoppable!"

"Yes, well, if we could do it without touching, it would be even better. That shock is not a pleasant feeling. Let's leave it for the more *knowledgeable* to train us instead of experimenting anymore, please," she said rubbing her hands. "The dark path it is."

Alric looked at her sharply, "how do you know that?"

"That other one is a dead end."

"Yes... but how do *you* know that? I hadn't said it out loud yet."

"Alric, I don't need you to dictate everything to me you know. Unless it's another illusion, I could see the dead end clear as day."

"You could *see* it?"

"Yes, Alric! Are you hard of hearing as well as bossy? I could, oh, OH! You shared your gift with me! That's... but... HOW?"

"I don't know. Let's hurry so the more *knowledgeable* can train us." He laughed and they headed toward the dark path.

"A little light, sister dear." She rolled her eyes, but stepped forward and pushed a flame to the palm of her right hand. This she could do easily. She found her right side to be dominant while Alric favored his left. They walked on, with no sign of it being day or night as they were surrounded by constant darkness. It was no wonder many never made it to Shama. Without gifts to rely on, the dark path would be the least likely chosen. The farther they walked, the narrower the path became. Soon they were walking single file, then sideways.

"Alric, are you sure this is right?" The wall was scraping and squeezing them more and more.

"You tell me," Alric grunted, "you saw it the same as I did. Wait!" Both of them froze in place.

"Do you feel that?"

"Yes! Hurry Alric! HURRY!"

They could feel the walls moving ever so slightly closer with each breath they took, no wonder they were having such a hard time walking. They were close to being squashed! Just when they thought they could take no more of the pressing and would never get out, they reached the other end and took several deep breaths. Looking back they could see the two sides of the wall close completely.

"Now I know how grapes feel!" Alric said, stretching his arms above his head.

Elainea looked around and found the stones shaped like a crown. There was no second marker offering directions like before.

"At least there are only three paths this time." Alric said before he again used his sight to eliminate one route. The other two seemed blocked to him somehow. They did not want to try joining again because it would tire them too much, and as they did not know what challenges lay ahead they wanted to conserve their energy.

"Elainea, try using sound. Like bats do."

She looked at him to see if he was serious. They had tried it several times during the journey and it was not something she was good with. It required an extreme amount of focus and silence to hear the return sounds.

She sent a short burst of sound, as high pitched as she could manage into one path, straining to hear its echo. Then, repeated the cry down the other path. One came back fairly quickly, meaning it was a dead end, the other echoed further away. Meaning there was an opening.

"Down the middle."

The path twisted and turned so much they quickly grew disoriented. It felt like they went backwards just as much as forwards. Sometimes they traveled on a steep incline and on other parts they slid downhill.

By the time they reached the end of that path, they were both breathing heavily and feeling hopelessly lost. The air was much thinner, so they must have traveled to a great height. The crags and clouds still blocked any view, but they assumed they had to have been halfway up the mountain. They had come to another opening, and were now faced with two paths. Snow had begun to fall and their teeth chattered as they contemplated which route to take. They could feel the temperature dropping with each moment and the wind whipped around them brutally. They had to yell just to be heard.

"We could make camp here and wait till morning."

"We have no idea when morning is, Elainea, and there is no wood to start a fire. I don't think you can keep us both warm long enough to reach our destination. Can you give me your cloak and warm yourself? We really must continue."

Elainea passed him her cloak and focused on the heat in her

belly. It grew and spread outward until she was warm enough to continue.

"Let's decide on the path quickly, before you freeze. You are too large for me to carry."

They agreed on the path to the left, as it appeared to slope upwards while the other went downwards. They started at a brisk pace and bounced right back. There was a barrier, of some sort, blocking the path. No, not a barrier.

"Another illusion" Alric said, rubbing his forehead where it had made contact. "This is a solid wall, the opposite of the first one we encountered by the river. Let's go down the other way."

They headed toward the right, only to bounce off of that one too.

"This can't be right." Elainea moaned. "One of them has to be the way to go." She could see the ice forming crystals on Alric's hair. It would soon be too cold for him to survive. She would be able to keep him warm in short bursts, but eventually her magic would tire out and they would both freeze.

Alric took a step back, it took all his concentration to focus past his freezing body to use his sight. When he did, it showed a single path directly before them. He was so cold and tired he didn't bother to explain to Elainea. Shivering, he grabbed her sleeve and pulled her toward the wall and then through it.

They stepped into a world that left them speechless.

"Welcome travelers. Enter and be refreshed," said a man garbed in a white robe. He had a long beard, and his dark hair had been braided and wrapped around his head like a crown. He stood with his bare feet deep in grass, greener than they had ever seen. Gazing around, they saw that they stood in a valley that was nestled in a cleft of the mountain range.

"Come! Come! We have much to discuss. The One and I have been watching and awaiting your arrival." His smile shone like pearls against his ebony complexion. The siblings followed him into a small cottage. Neither said a word, so in awe were they.

"Please remove your shoes. This is a sacred place, and it will help with your training to really *feel* the energy."

They did as he asked before entering his home. Still, they could not speak. Somehow, they both knew what they would learn and encounter there would be far greater than anything they had imagined.

Chapter 28

LADY DEVONA SAT AT HER DRESSING table staring at her reflection. She smiled. She expected a knock on her door at any minute, servants coming to tell her the king had tragically died in his sleep. She would feign devastation and mournfully take up the mantle in his stead. She would be strong for her people. She almost giggled at her own genius.

A knock sounded, "Come in."

"Mother! Lovely to see you this morning. Why the dark colors though? Are you in mourning perhaps?" The dark ring had almost completely covered his eyes, only the barest glimmer of blue was still visible.

"My King! I was not expecting you. How... how may I be of service?" Devona was in shock. He should not be standing there. He should be dead! What had she done wrong? Even worse, did he know about her attempt on his life?

"I was thinking of your offer and have found a way for you to prove your loyalty. As you know, we have signed alliances with Vimeo, and their neighbors. I think you would be a perfect envoy to ensure everything goes as planned." He grinned at her, "don't you agree?"

"That is a brilliant idea, my King. Who better to look after your interest than your mother?"

"My thoughts exactly. You leave in a fortnight."

"So quickly?"

"Why, do you have more pressing matters to attend to here?"

"No, no, I was only thinking of packing so many dresses." She said limply.

"I'm sure you were. And just in case you are less than thrilled about your upcoming departure, you'll have a guard assigned to you at all times." He walked to the door and paused at the threshold,

"Oh, and Mother?"

"Yes?"

"You must give me the recipe for that cake you made." He winked at her, "it was delicious."

His manic laughter echoed down the hall, making her tremble from head to toe.

King David sauntered to Chumbra's room and entered without knocking.

"Your Majesty. How may I serve you today?"

"Chumbra, my good man. You have already served me more than you know. The spell you placed on me to detect poisons worked better than I expected."

"My King! Who would dare try to poison you?"

"Oh, no surprise really, it was my mother. It seems to be a habit of hers. But never mind that, she will be leaving us for Vimeo shortly. Let her take her machinations and pester them there for a while."

"Wonderful idea, Your Majesty. Is there anything else I can do for you?"

"Yes, I would like a spell placed on this necklace. The butterfly that is encased in amber, can you make it animate so it can free itself and deliver messages to me? I want to know everything that is going on in Vimeo and... blast, I can never remember the name of that other country! No matter, can it be done?"

"Hmm, give me some time to consult my books, Your Majesty. I am sure I can find a solution to fit your needs."

"Very well. This necklace is a gift for Sybella, to show I harbor no ill will for her jilting me. Mother will hand deliver it so it must be ready when she leaves in a fortnight."

"As you wish, Your Majesty."

Chapter 29

CHUMBRA POURED OVER HIS BOOKS and scrolls, finally finding a spell that would suit the king's purpose. He knew Sybella was not a frivolous woman. While she was quite pretty, she did not fancy pretty baubles and dresses. She was practical and very mannish in her mannerisms. A necklace would be tossed aside and gather none of the information the king would want. No, it would have to be something she would actually carry on her person.

He walked to the treasury and glanced around. A dagger would be too suspicious, a necklace like the king suggested would be discarded. All the jewelry he saw was extravagant and would never do. He continued to look around and landed on a set of earrings. They were flat discs, hammered to a high shine. Small enough to be unobtrusive, yet pretty and plain enough to appeal to her. This he could use, by spelling them they could be linked to one of the king's mirrors and in essence become a spy glass. The king would see almost whatever the wearer saw and hear whatever the wearer heard. He took them back to his room to begin the process.

Lord Vicrano watched from the docks as his men loaded the rest of the items necessary to work on the river pass onto his fleet of ships. It would take them two days, if the weather held, to reach the shores of Elhaanai. And King David was sending his mother as an envoy when they were to return. Envoy, spy more like it. But he would play along, after all he had been spying on them for far longer.

Sybella approached with her husband, Ashrek, in tow.

"Ahh Sybella, Ashrek, Welcome. As you can see, we are well into the river pass construction. Have you started your tunnel yet Ashrek?"

"No, I haven't. I have yet to find a suitable starting point. The mountain is unstable in many areas and to begin shifting stone could cause an avalanche and the loss of many lives. I will keep searching. Sybella has told me how vital this route will be for future generations." He gazed at his wife with adoration. Sybella blushed from under her lashes, looking at him demurely. If Vicrano did not know her, he would have been fooled as well.

"Very good. Sybella, when will we be returning the gift to Lord Alcherist?"

"It will be dealt with at once, Father, as soon as I return to the manor. I believe they have learned their lesson, there should be no relapses."

"Perfect, we shall keep an eye on them, nonetheless. One can never be too trusting."

♕

From the nursery, Lord Alcherist watched the sun set on yet another day without his son. It had been weeks! His rage simmered just beneath the surface; he would have his vengeance for this injustice. The pain this had caused his wife was unforgivable.

He turned to leave and caught the scent of sulfur and heard a slight pop from behind him. He turned and barely caught sight of an evil grin before it vanished in a puff of black smoke. When the noxious fumes cleared, his son lay asleep in his crib!

He ran to his side and scooped him into his arms. Tears of joy streamed down his cheeks as he embraced the child who squirmed against the tight hold. He rushed off to his own room and found his wife forlornly sitting by the hearth. He approached with a soft tread and knelt before her, placing the child in her lap. At first, she made no move and seemed not to recognize him, but when the child reached up for her, she awoke from her stupor and clasped him to her chest with a gut-wrenching sob. She rocked him back and forth, crying with relief. Mother and child stayed that way through the night. Alcherist watched over them as they slept, plotting his revenge from the shadows.

Lord Overton was over the moon at the news his nephew had finally been returned. His son, Ashrek, had not been able to gather much information without revealing his duplicitous position. He needed to keep Vicrano believing that he was besotted with Sybella. Their time would come, and until then he would keep his brother from doing anything rash. He had not included him in his plans and for good reason. He was too emotional, too slow in making the hard but necessary decisions, and he could not see the bigger picture. Alcherist would thank him when the dust settled, and the hierarchy was as it should be.

<h1 style="text-align:center">Chapter 30</h1>

AKRONIUS AND NAIA MADE THEIR WAY down the river toward the mountain ridge. Though the youths he was tracking had tried to hide their trail, he was a master at his craft. He had hoped the wolf would be able to pick up their scent, but he realized she had never met them. Winter had them firmly in its grasp and the river was partially frozen over. He picked a large tree to shelter them from the wind and falling snow. It had been hollowed out and he hoped the inhabitants were no longer present. On closer inspection, there was evidence of a large fire. He guessed the kids had sheltered here at some point. The girl had the gift over fire, she must have tried to start a fire and things got a bit out of control. There were bits of charred cloth embedded into the inside of the tree. He laughed to himself, trial by fire I suppose. They seem to have taken the time on the journey to practice their gifts, if they continued to be this inept it would be easy to track them.

His thoughts traveled back to his many conversations with Wleia about her children. The boy, Alric, had the gift of sight like Queen Alanna along with the gift of telekinesis and shields. The girl, Elainea, had the gift of fire and alchemy with a touch of a botanical gift. Wleia said it was almost as if she could speak to the plants. She somehow knew where to find each herb and how mixing each item would interact with the others. Wleia had even expressed a theory; she believed the twins could share their gifts with each other. If that were the case, they would be the most powerful people since Elrond; even more powerful than Queen Alanna and King Kaison had been.

Akronius had not been born with any true gifting; he had honed his skills as a swordsman, while perfecting his ability to track. That was why he was so often sent on secret missions by Devona. Queen Alanna had told him his methods had been too violent, given his childhood how could they blame him. Still they were the King and

Queen so outwardly he had remained loyal to the throne but inwardly had strayed to Devona. Not too long ago he and Devona had been kindred spirits. He rubbed Naia's head absentmindedly. Things had definitely changed. He gazed out of the trunk of the tree at the snow whirling around. He silently asked for guidance and wisdom. He did not want to end up tossed to and fro like those flakes, he wanted to be sure of his path. His life depended on it!

Devona made one last pass through her room, making sure she had everything she would need in the coming days or weeks. She had no idea how long her son would have her stay as envoy to the allied nations; envoy was just a diplomatic way of saying banishment. He was sending her directly into a nest of vipers and she would have to adapt or die. Devona had become increasingly comfortable with the serpentine nature she was developing; adapting was a way of life for her. David may, yet, live to regret sending her away.

"Knock, knock. Ready Mother?" King David asked sarcastically from her doorway. Devona turned toward him with a forced smile.

"Yes, Your Majesty. I look forward to the change in scenery. I will not let you down."

"I am sure you won't." David looked at her suspiciously. He knew she wanted him dead, that she wanted to ascend the throne herself. He thought sending her away would rid him of that problem. Suddenly, he wasn't so sure, she was so self-confident; like she knew something he did not, and that made him very uneasy. He needed to keep an eye on her while also keeping her far enough away that she could not stab him in the back. Luckily, Chumbra had completed the spyglass spell and he would have eyes and ears on her at all times.

"Mother, please take this and present it as a gift to Sybella as a sign that I bear no ill will toward her over the failed arrangement between us. Let her know, I wish them only the best and hope our two countries will remain allies for the foreseeable future."

They stood just outside the manor waiting for the carriage to arrive that would take them to the docks for her impending departure.

"How very diplomatic of you. I will deliver your message. We really mustn't keep Lord Vicrano waiting any longer. I understand all the workers have been offloaded and he is eager to return home." Lady Devona turned her back on the king, since she knew it irritated him. She barely suppressed the urge to laugh as a small growl slipped past his kingly facade.

"You are right. Let us be on our way then."

He stepped to her side and offered his hand to assist her into the carriage. They rode in silence to the docks and Devona boarded the ship without a glance back. The king made eye contact with Lord Vicrano as he stood on the deck and the barest of nods were exchanged. Lord Vicrano watched the king ride away in his heavily-ornate conveyance and shook his head. Many believed you could not direct the tides, but if you dropped a large enough boulder in a pool at exactly the right spot, the waves would carry you to exactly where you wanted to be.

Chapter 31

SHAMA WATCHED THE TWO YOUNG PEOPLE with curiosity. He could see the power flowing all around them. It moved and jumped from one to the other like a living, breathing thing. Red flames, white mist, green vines, blue orbs and a subtle silver undertone to each color. It was an amazing sight. And yet, every so often there seemed to be a void, a darkness that swallowed the other colors. He had read of this in his scrolls, but never had he witnessed it. It took a physical effort to mask the fear of what this meant. He would have to look into this at a later time. If he was correct, dark times were fast approaching and an old relic would soon make a reappearance.

"Would you like any more to eat Alric? Elainea?"

"No thank you Sir. It was… wait, how do you know our names?" Alric asked.

"I told you Son, we have been waiting for you. For both of you. Now come, I will show you to your rooms where you can refresh yourselves. Your training will begin at once."

The rooms were modest but homey. There was a cot with warm bedding, and a dressing table with a basin for washing. Elainea noticed no mirror. Everything was made of wood so there were no reflective surfaces anywhere. Strangely enough there was no actual floor. The ground was literally earth. A thick carpet of lush grass was in every room and down every hallway. Shama had said it would help them connect to their gifts. Time would tell, but at least it was comfortable.

Once they were settled in, they all returned to the courtyard.

"Shama, may I ask a question?"

"You already have. But feel free to ask another," he said with an infectious smile.

"Why are there no mirrors or any reflective surfaces?"

"I am glad you noticed. It shows you are aware of your

surroundings. A characteristic you will both need in the future. There are no reflective surfaces because, here, you have no need to inspect your outward selves. We will be focused on what lies within. There is no natural mirror that can reveal that."

"Now, I will tell you what I know and what has been revealed to me during my walks with The One. Alric, you have the gift of sight, shields and telekinesis. Elainea, you can control fire and understand herbs and spells. Am I correct?"

They both nodded.

"I have the gift of sight as well, but not the same as yours Alric. In each gift there are variations. You can see distances and through objects, your mother could see through objects, animate or not, and also through lies. I can see gifts, or rather the essence of gifts. Each one has a different color. Red is for fire or heat. Blue is for water or telekinesis. White is for sight or air, and green for spells or earth. Each gift can be one thing or the other, and sometimes even both. Even rarer still is silver. This gift is only present in true soul mates, like your genetic parents Alric, or very powerful siblings. I think you two will fall into that latter category. When I first saw you, there was a thin thread of silver weaving between all your gifts. It is not always visible, which means it is weak. We will work to strengthen that and all your other gifts."

Alric and Elainea looked at each other in excitement.

"What does the silver mean?" Elainea asked.

"Silver is the ability to share one's gift or telepathy. Your parents could speak telepathically Alric. I assume you cannot as siblings. You should be able to share your gifts with each other."

"Yes, we can! We held hands on our journey here and it shocked us. That first time I lost control of my fire and he lost control of his telekinesis. He ended up with a few burn marks and I was thrown quite a distance."

"That is amazing! The fact that you would even attempt it says much about your strength and fortitude. We will work on each of you recognizing the feel of your individual gifts so you can recognize it in each other and draw from it. You will need this ability in the future. I will push you to the very end of your strength and then beyond. Resistance will make it harder. You need to trust me even

when what I ask seems to make no sense to you.”
    “We understand.”
    “Let’s begin.”

Chapter 32

AT THE BASE OF THE MOUNTAIN, work was well underway on the river pass. Men worked through the heat of the day and then by lamplight through the night. At the current pace, King David and Lord Vicrano would have the road completed in less than a month's time. No one understood why they were in such a rush. The men were driven at an unbearable pace, and if they fell behind, they were thrown into the dungeon and replaced by someone else. Mothers hid their sons or sent them south. Every male, fifteen years of age and older was sent to work on the road.

The king was going over final plans with his advisors when there was a knock on the door. "Enter!"

"Your Highness, Chumbra has requested an audience with you," a servant said quietly.

"Send him in."

"Your Highness, thank you so much for seeing me on such short notice."

"What do you want, Chumbra?"

"I need more… volunteers. My studies are producing the results you requested, but it would go much faster if I had more bodies." Chumbra looked around the room at the advisors; he knew none of them would question the king directly. None had an inkling of what the king had requested of him.

Shortly after Lady Devona was sent away, Chumbra had approached the king with a proposition.

"Your Highness, forgive my boldness. I am very glad that the spell I provided was able to detect the poison your mother intended for you. I wonder if I could offer my services in another capacity?"

"Yes Chumbra, it was fortunate that you knew of that spell. What did you have in mind?"

"My King, it is well known that many of your subjects grumble against you

Now, it was a weekly occurrence for grief-stricken family members to wait at the gate for the guardsman to post a list of names of all those who had died mysteriously while in custody. And if their names were not posted, guards would claim ignorance of having ever arrested the individual. Weeping and wailing had replaced the laughter that once sounded in the streets.

Chumbra walked through the dungeon, glancing left and right for what he was looking for as if he were in the marketplace. When he first started visiting the dank place, he had promised freedom for those who voluntarily offered their assistance. Since then, the inhabitants had learned that whoever went with Chumbra either never returned, or came back missing body parts. They shrank from the bars of their cells, trying to make themselves invisible to his calculating stare.

He stopped at a cell and pointed, "that one." The guards pushed and prodded their way into the cell as if they were moving a herd of cattle and dragged the woman kicking and screaming from her hiding place. Chumbra placed his thumb on her forehead, leaving behind a sticky smudge and she was silenced immediately.

"Much better," he sighed. He began walking and she followed mutely behind, eyes darting to the left and right, wide with fear but her body unable to fight the command from the spell placed on her. Chumbra led her to a staircase that wound its way up into the manor and into a secret room behind his chambers. Here, he could do as he pleased. He had also spelled the walls so the screams could not be heard.

"Lay on the table." She did, and he placed restraints on her as the spell he had placed was only temporary. Chumbra needed her to be conscious for what he had planned today. It would wear off shortly and he would begin the extraction. He had kept all the virgins grouped together for just this purpose. He glanced at his notebooks and confirmed the next step.

As he read, he sharpened his blade on a sandstone. While the sound soothed him, it inspired terror in those he worked on. He could tell by the moans that escalated to screaming that the spell had finally worn off. He would use no anesthetic as it weakened the purity of the blood. Her screams reached an octave that curled his toes with pleasure as he slid the blade across her abdomen to remove her womb.

Chumbra surveyed the girl on the table. Blood had been collected in various jars and her womb placed in a sacred vessel for later use. He watched as her breathing slowed and her eyes glossed over. He captured her last breath in a special bladder made from the skin of a newborn lamb. Finally, he had almost everything he needed for what his master desired. Only one last ingredient was needed. He would have to plan very carefully how to retrieve it.

<h1 style="text-align:center">Chapter 33</h1>

AKRONIUS WAS FINALLY WITHIN SIGHT of the mountain. Soon he could hear the thunder of the raging falls. This is where things would become tricky, construction on the king's bridge was happening not too far away so it would be extremely difficult to sneak by without being noticed. It would also be difficult to track the children in the mountains. He had removed bits of cloth from the scorched tree in hopes that Naia would be able to scent it for him. He was able to follow slight markers, indenting in the soft mud of a boot print, the crushing of a weed, they all showed him where the narrow path was that led behind the falls. He waited until nightfall and then cautiously proceeded. Once behind the falls, he was able to release the breath he held and gave Naia a good whiff of the rags and hoped all the moisture in the air wouldn't dampen her sense of smell.

Naia sniffed around for a few minutes before that same urging, she had felt when her woman was sick caught her again. She had to run, but the man must follow. She yipped and ran to him then back to the spot on the wall that called her. He seemed to sense her meaning for he came quickly this time. She paused only slightly before jumping through what looked like a wall, the man on her heels.

"Well, I'll be! Good job Naia." He looked around and saw four possible paths. "Which way Naia?" His faith in her strengthened the tug she felt, and off she raced down the dark path. It was very narrow and her sides were scraped when she got through. Each route was as clear as if a beacon lit her way. Finally, they reached the last fork in the road but something was wrong. Naia no longer felt the tugging, she went to each path and found it blocked. Whining, she turned to the man for help.

"You did good Naia. Now it's my turn." He walked to one path and then the other feeling the walls. "These paths are both illusions so that leaves me thinking the true path should also be covered by an illusion." Akronius began feeling along the wall from left to right. When he reached the middle of the path, he fell straight through and landed with his face deep in lush grass. Looking up he came face to face with his quarry. Their look quickly transitioned from surprise to fear and then an intense anger.

"What are you doing here?" All the restraint Alric had been practicing flew right over the cliff face. Behind him, Elainea stood with a scowl on her face and white-hot flames in both palms. At that moment, Naia bounded through the rock face and landed in front of him, fangs bared.

"Peace. Everyone please, calm down." Shama walked calmly between the two parties. He turned first to Alric, simply raising one eyebrow. Alric closed his eyes and took a deep breath. Elainea doused her flames and stood shoulder to shoulder with her brother, still glaring at Akronius. From behind Shama a whine was heard. He turned and knelt before the wolf.

"Well done Naia. You and your master." Naia growled and Shama chuckled. "My apologies, you and Akronius are the final part of the training of my charges. You are both welcome here."

"Shama, may we speak, privately, please?" Alric spoke through clenched teeth. He was trembling from the effort it took to control his anger.

Wleia had said he would appear amicable, Akronius thought, if this was amicable, he was as good as dead.

"No, you may not. But thank you for asking so politely. We all know who he was and what he has done. What you do not know is who he is now and what he will do in the future." He turned to Akronius, "come, there is something that must be done before you can continue on your journey."

Akronius looked at Elainea and then turned to face Alric. Locking eyes, Akronius bowed from the waist, "I will take my leave now, Your Majesty." Alric tried to hide his surprise but Elainea's gasp beside him spoiled his efforts.

Shama smiled and led Akronius away.

"Elainea, he knows who I am."

"And Shama knew that he knew who you were. Something

must have changed. We should at least hear him out... Your Majesty." Elainea elbowed Alric in the side.

"Hey, you're supposed to bow to me! I'll have you flayed you peasant!" Alric followed his sister into the cottage. He gazed back to see Akronius follow Shama around a bend. He trusted Shama implicitly. He would have to be patient and see what the future held.

Akronius followed Shama down a rocky path, nearly losing his footing several times. He looked around but couldn't see anything through the clouds, there was nothing to discern whether it was day or night.

"Akronius, you have lived a hard life. You have done a great many evil things, including murdering Alric's mother, Queen Alanna."

"Yes, I have." Akronius did not try to deny the truth.

"You have also had a change of heart recently."

"That is also true."

The two men stopped at a pool surrounded by large black rocks. Shama turned and looked at Akronius.

"Look into the pool and tell me what you see."

Chapter 34

HESITANTLY, AKRONIUS STEPPED FORWARD and gazed at his reflection.   His eyes widened and he stepped back, shaken to his core.

"Akronius, what did you see?"

"My, it was me, but…" Akronius bowed his head and his shoulders sagged.   "It was my reflection covered in the blood of those I have killed.   My eyes were black as tar and my teeth were razor sharp."

"Yes, Akronius.   That was your reflection.   Do you want it to be a prediction as well?"   Akronius shook his head.   "Then step into the pool."

Akronius looked again at the pool.   Instead of the tranquil surface of a moment ago, it bubbled and roiled as if a great fire raged beneath the surface.   With uncertainty, he placed one foot in and then the other. He turned to Shama for instructions.

"Submerge yourself."

Akronius could not swim.   His breath came in short spurts as he took another step forward.   The water rose to his knees, then his waist.   The next step plunged him in up to his neck and he cried out in fear.   A whisper floated through the air, 'STRONG AND COURAGEOUS'.   He closed his eyes and took a deep shuddering breath and took the final step.   The water rushed over his head and he struggled not to panic as he began to sink.   He felt something hit him in the chest and he fought to keep what little air he had inside. He opened his eyes in time to see a current travel at full speed toward him as he was hit again, harder this time, forcing all the air from his lungs in a painful rush.   He began to thrash around, reaching for the surface that should have been just above him but wasn't.   His vision began to dim and his thrashing turned to spasms as he fought not to inhale.   When he could no longer resist, he gave up and took a deep breath, and then another. How was this possible? He looked around him. He was floating in what seemed to be water, but he could breath as if he stood on the shore. He looked above him and saw the rippling silhouette of Shama, he looked below and there was no bottom. Strangely enough, he was not afraid. He felt a tingling sensation begin in his fingers and toes that traveled up his legs and down his arms. It grew in intensity until it reached his core, filling him until he felt like he would explode. He felt himself being lifted and wrapped in warmth like a mother's embrace. And like a butterfly emerging from a cocoon, he stretched and opened his eyes to find himself prostrate on the shore of the pool that was once again smooth as glass.

"Look into the pool, Akronius."

Akronius made his way to the pool and gasped at his reflection, he was *clean*! Not only that, but a golden aura shone around him. It moved as if it were alive; wrapping itself around him, disappearing into his body, only to reappear from another point. He turned to Shama. "What is this? What does this mean?"

"It means Akronius that The One has forgiven you, and claimed you as his own. Your gift has awakened. It is one that has not been seen since King Kronius, and before him. It has been a hundred years since it has appeared. It is unconventional, be careful to use it wisely."

"But what is my gift exactly?"

"Follow me."

They traveled back on the same path but everything looked different to Akronius. Colors were sharper, scents were stronger and there was so much noise. The closer they came to the courtyard, the more conversations he heard.

"Shama, is it always this busy here? I thought your home was hard to find."

Shama only laughed and turned the corner into the courtyard. "Busy? We are the only ones here Akronius, look around you."

Akronius turned in a full circle and though he saw no other people, save Alric and Elainea, he could hear multiple conversations. He tried to narrow in on the closest one.

"Did you get everything you needed to start building? The weather is changing and we will have to build soon."

"Yes, yes, yes! Don't I always? Every year you peck at me! Leave me be!"

The closer Akronius got to the conversation, the more convinced he was that he had drowned in that pool. He simply could not believe his eyes or ears. He stood in front of a tree and two blue jays twittered back and forth around a half-built nest. If he focused, he could hear words, when he moved the voices to the background of his mind, they sounded like normal birds.

"HA!" Akronius barked, startling both birds into taking flight. He spun quickly and found Shama smiling at him, "unconventional huh? Does it go both ways?"

"I should think so."

Akronius approached Naia as she lay by Alric's side. "Pardon me Your Highness, but perhaps you should move a bit further away from that she-wolf. She has fleas."

Naia sat up and grunted. "I most certainly do *not* have fleas, you ingrate! He should distance himself from you! How the woman tolerated your foul smell is beyond me."

"Ha, ha, ha!" Akronius guffawed, "I do not smell Naia. In fact, I am the cleanest I have ever been."

"Says you. Wait, you can understand me?" Naia moved to sit on her haunches and cocked her head to the side.

"Oh yes. I most definitely can!"

"Great! Now I will have to be more mindful of what I say." Naia huffed, plopped herself back down and closed her eyes.

"SHAMA, this is amazing! Now my natural tracking and fighting skills make sense. Thank you, thank you!"

"Do not thank me, Akronius. Thank The One who gave it to you. Only the worthy are given gifts such as you three possess." Shama said, while staring pointedly at Alric. "Come, we have much to discuss and hard conversations are always better when spoken over tea and cookies."

<h1 style="text-align:center">Chapter 35</h1>

ONCE THEY WERE ALL SETTLED around the table, Shama addressed them as one. "What will be spoken at this table will be hard to hear for you, Alric and you, Elainea. It will also be hard to say Akronius. But you must work through the pain to reach common ground. It is necessary for the survival of all of us. My one rule, you are not to interrupt the one speaking." He looked pointedly at Elainea as she had trouble with this rule. "Everyone will have a chance to ask questions and find answers." Shama took a deep breath and looked to Akronius, "the arrow must be pulled from the wound before healing can start. You will begin."

Akronius shifted uncomfortably on his cushion. The table they sat around was low to the ground. He met Alric's hard stare and knew Shama was right.

"Twenty years ago, your aunt, Lady Devona poisoned your father and charged me and my men with killing your mother, who carried you in her womb at the time. We formed a small group of skilled men and stormed her chamber. We thought she was reclining in her bed, but when the arrows simply passed through her, we knew it was an illusion. Queen Alanna had managed to slip out of the manor via a secret passage and escape from us, for a time. When we caught up with her, we cornered her at the river. It was raging from runoff and she could not cross it. My men surrounded her and fired their crossbows. She was powerful but weak, and the shield she erected was slow enough that one arrow pierced her back and went through into her belly. I taunted her as she lay dying, and she left my face marked as you see now. My men and I left her to die. Only she didn't. We later learned that she had made her way to the barn of a widow named Wleia. A spell was performed and you survived. I suppose you know most of what has happened between that time and the day you started your journey here, except for the role I played in it."

Akronius looked to Shama for encouragement; this would be painful for both Alric and Elainea. "When Devona learned through the Oracle that you still lived, she sent me on a hunt for you. We did meet that one time in the market. You recognized me, Alric, but I did not know who you were, and I am glad of that fact now. I spent several more weeks in your village, only to learn too late that you had left. I made my way to your farm and…"

"You better not have hurt my mother!" Elainea interrupted.

"You have broken my one rule." Shama held his hand over her cup and it glowed a bright white, "Drink!"

Elainea sighed and lifted the cup to her lips. She was well acquainted with her punishment. The tea would take her voice for the remainder of the night. She would have no choice but to listen to the rest of this confessional.

"I did not hurt Wleia, in fact it was quite the opposite. In an attempt to spy and learn as much about both of you as I could, I forced myself into her good graces. I stayed at your farm for a month and in that time, your mother, Wleia, changed my life. I returned empty handed to the manor house ready to have my life ended for my failure. That end was avoided because David had taken over the throne. There was a darkness that had settled over the place, things were not as I had left them. King David gave me a new mission. I was to come here and should I find you, my orders were to kill you and Shama. I had no intention of doing that, not after learning so much about both of you from Wleia. It felt like we were family, something I never had. Several things happened before I began tracking you here, the most important of which is Wleia. Naia came to find me, she had run until her paws bled. She never left Wleia's side, *never!* I followed her back and found your mother very sick. She had taken a bad fall and the bone did not set properly. I nursed her as best as I could, I promise. There is nothing I would not have done for her… but I could not save her." Tears were falling down the faces of Alric, Elainea and Akronius. Naia whimpered in the corner and laid her head on Akronius' knee in solidarity. She missed her too. "Every morning she watched the sunrise over the mountain and every evening she watched it set and said a prayer for The One to guide and protect you. She is buried facing the mountain. Her last request of me was to find and protect you, to help you regain your place on the throne. I promised her that I would. Naia helped me track you, and here I am, humbly at your service, Your Majesty."

Alric placed his head in his hands, breathing deeply. He wiped tears off his face. His sister sat weeping silently beside him and he gathered her into his arms. Her inability to audibly grieve made it all the worse. Finally, she rose and walked out of the room, hunched over with her arms wrapped tightly around herself as if she would fall to pieces if she let go. He would find her in much the same way later that night, rocking silently back and forth on her bed.

Alric looked at Akronius. He was at a loss for words. This man had been there at the death of both of his mothers. One he caused, and the other he was witness to. How could he tell if what he said was true? How could he learn to trust him?

"Shama, it is said that animals are the best at judging the true nature of a man. Is it possible that I could share the gift Akronius has, and speak to Naia? She has spent the most time with him."

"Yes, Alric, it is possible, but it will be very difficult. You will have to lay your soul open to him as he will to you. The golden glow of this particular gift is tied to the soul of the animal. Understand?" Both men nodded, "Good. Alric, come sit beside Akronius. Akronius, please ask Naia to sit between you. Now both of you place your hands on her."

Alric gasped as the warmth of the connection flowed through him.

"Naia, can you understand me?"

"Yes, I can. We wolves are much smarter than those mutts you humans spend so much time with. Ask your questions."

"Is what he says true? Is my mother dead?"

Naia whimpered and lowered her head. "Yes, she has left this world. She was in great pain until this man came to help. He is arrogant, but has a kind heart. At least he does now. When he first came to us, he was covered in the stench of darkness. Your mother found me when my own mother was killed by hunters. She spoke of you often and with great affection. She spoke to him as well. What he says is true. He is not a wolf, but he is part of my pack, as your mother was.”

Akronius ruffled the top of her head affectionately and she snapped at him playfully before walking outside, breaking the connection.

“Have your doubts been assuaged, Alric?” Shama gently asked.

“Yes, they have. Thank you.” He turned his gaze to Akronius, “What now?”

“After we convince your sister not to roast me tomorrow, we make you king.”

“You make it sound so easy.”

“You’ll make a great king Alric, I am…”

“Not that part! My sister is very good with a flame and very stubborn!” Both men laughed and clasped forearms in solidarity.

Chapter 36

LADY DEVONA LOOKED AROUND HER ROOM with loathing. She was in a high room with a guard stationed outside the door. The hearth had not been cleaned of ashes and dust lay on every surface. She looked at the bed and shuddered, how long was she to remain here? She whipped around as the door flew open.

"Don't you barbarians knock before, oh, Priestess Sybella, my apologies." Devona bowed her head respectfully.

"No, no Lady Devona. My apologies. I am not used to the feminine politeness as you are. I go where I please, when I please around here. Perhaps you could help me with that?" Sybella looked around, "and I can help you with this room."

Devona watched curiously as Sybella raised her arms and began chanting while moving them in a pattern. Her eyes blackened completely and her voice took on a raspy sound. She clapped once and dust flew around them so quickly, Devona had to cover her eyes. When she opened them, everything was pristine. There was a roaring fire in the hearth and heavy drapes on each post of the bed. Devona looked at Sybella in awe!

"You are well versed in the dark arts. I would be happy to help you in any way if you would agree to teach me even a little of what you know, and before I forget," Devona rushed to retrieve the gift from David. "My son, King David, sends this gift to you to show he bears no ill will on the broken engagement and to wish you happiness in your marriage."

Sybella opened the small box and tilted her head to look at the earrings. "I'll admit I'm not one who wears jewelry for beauty alone. All of my charms serve a purpose for our dark lord. But these are simple enough. I'll send my thanks to the king. Now, dinner is being prepared. Would you care to join my family or would you prefer to stay here and rest? We can have the meal brought to you."

Lady Devona smiled, "I would love to join you for dinner. Lead the way."

The two women made their way down the narrow staircase to the banqueting hall, chatting pleasantly. Devona had heard so many evil things about this girl that she was wondering if they were all lies. When they reached the hall, Lord Vicrano was already seated at the head of the table along with a man she did not know.

"Ahh Lady Devona! So nice of you to join us for dinner. Please have a seat and let me introduce you to Lord Ashrek, Sybella's husband and son of Lord Overton." Vicrano said the last part with a smile, watching Devona closely for the moment she realized the marriage had been one of political benefit and not children running off to be wed in secret, as he had told her.

Lady Devona locked eyes with Lord Vicrano and smiled. "Lord Ashrek, how nice to finally meet the man who stole Sybella from my son. You must be quite special."

"Not at all Lady Devona, Sybella is the special one. I was just fortunate enough to catch her eye." Ashrek gazed lovingly at his wife who blushed under his stare.

Lady Devona smiled but was not fooled. She would spend time with them, but she would not let down her guard. She had no doubt that Lord Vicrano was up to something, she just had to determine what it was and whether Sybella and Ashrek were part of the plot. She turned to her meal and finished it completely, it was pleasant enough, though it was an acquired taste.

"Lady Devona, I do hope you enjoyed your meal. It is a delicacy here in Vimeo. I understand in Elhaanai, blood is cleansed from meat prior to cooking. Here we value the power found in it and it is an ingredient in all our cooking." Sybella said quietly.

Devona visibly paled as she stared down at her empty plate, feeling her stomach roll within her. She asked for pardon before bolting from her seat to a bowl placed conveniently nearby.

"Oh dear! I have upset you! I am so, so sorry, that was not my intention at all! Please let me have a maid escort you back to your room to rest." Sybella beckoned a maid and Devona leaned heavily on her as she exited. She glanced behind her to see a wicked grin on Sybella's face. Not lies after all.

"Now that you've had your fun Sybella, let's get to business." He turned to Ashrek, "where are you with the tunnel?"

"I have found the spot and will begin shifting it tomorrow morning. Perhaps you would like to come watch?"

"Perfect! And I will be right there to make sure everything goes accordingly. This is the first step of many."

"Yes, it is." Ashrek said with a smile.

Chapter 37

LADY DEVONA LAY IN HER ROOM still fighting the nausea brought on by that horrid meal. She would have to enlist someone to cook her meals from now on. She should have known better; food could never be trusted when surrounded by enemies. Sybella was a viper, but that was alright, she was not the only one with reptilian characteristics. She waited until she was sure the guard was asleep before she activated her gift. The transition was seamless, like stepping out of a dressing gown. She slowly opened the door and slid out. She made her way down the stairs to explore the rest of the manor. She could still hear voices in the dining hall. Lord Vicrano and Ashrek had their heads bent together whispering, though Sybella was not present.

She silently walked down the halls stopping every now and then to listen in on conversation. She discovered nothing she did not already suspect. Vicrano believed he should be king and had begun sending his people to Elhaanai to sow discontent among the people. The increase in vagrants that King David had chosen to ignore was the first wave of a well-planned coup. She needed to know how strong Vicrano was before she picked a side, son or not.

She silently explored the manor through the night, never once coming across Sybella. They must have secret rooms and passageways similar to the ones back home. When dawn was about to break, she crept back to her room. She silently closed the door, only to gasp in shock, seeing Sybella waiting by her bedside, her nightgown neatly folded and resting in her lap. What should she do? The choice was taken from her when Sybella said, "Lady Devona, welcome back. You must be positively frozen! I made you some tea and please get dressed." She smiled and motioned to the table where an open jewelry box sat next to a steaming cup of tea.

Devona did as she was asked and slipped back into her

nightgown when the transformation was complete. She turned and stared at Sybella, unsure what would come next.

"How did you know?"

"I am a priestess of the dark lord. Did you think you could come into *my* home and use dark gifts without me finding out? Tsk, tsk Devona, your old age is affecting your good senses. Your gift is not special nor will it be useful for whatever spying your son intended you to do."

"I see. So, will I be confined to this room?"

"Of course not! We are not so barbaric here. Violent, cunning and occasionally malicious but not barbaric. You can go almost anywhere you like with a guard. There are winter gardens and the menagerie holds some very interesting creatures. But if you can't find something to occupy your time, the dungeons are always an option."

"The gardens sound lovely."

"So glad we understand each other, I will leave you to your skinning then."

Sybella smiled as she left a fuming Devona behind her. Truthfully, were it not for the spies in Elhaanai, she would never have known Devona had such a gift. If she could figure out how to replicate it or turn Devona to their cause it would prove very useful.

The next morning, Ashrek and Lord Vicrano made their way to the base of the mountain where the tunnel would begin.

"This is the spot," Ashrek said. "You will want to stay behind me once I begin. I'll move farther into the tunnel and you can follow if you like."

"I want to see and be part of every step of this process. You have no idea how long we have been waiting for this." Lord Vicrano stepped back as Ashrek closed his eyes and lifted his hands. The ground began to shake and a distant rumble was heard. A perfect circle formed directly before Ashrek and slowly grew in size.

Lord Vicrano's eyes widened; it was amazing! Drops of sweat began pouring down Ashrek's face as he felt the weight of the mountain shifting with the widening of the tunnel. As it reached a man's' height, men rushed back and forth with support beams. Finally, Ashrek called out, "Enough!" He dropped to one knee in exhaustion.

"How long will you need to rest? How much further do we have to go?"

Ashrek's expression flashed from hatred to passive, in a blink of an eye. "I picked the shortest route I could, I need only an hour and we can begin again. At this pace we will be through to the other side by nightfall, barring a collapse."

"Is a collapse possible? You told me you picked the safest spot."

"And I did, but rocks are always unpredictable. I can channel through them, not see through them. Crevices and cracks could turn up anywhere."

Lord Vicrano eyed Ashrek's sweat-lined face as if searching for a lie. Men stood around them waiting for a word from them that the work would continue. Finally, he nodded in satisfaction. "Rest and let me know when you are ready to begin again." He walked off towards where the men continued to shore up the sides of the new tunnel.

Ashrek took a deep breath and walked to sit by a tree. The rocks around him trembled and burst into fine dust. He closed his eyes again and tried to center himself, suppressing the building rage. That is how Vicrano found him when it was time to begin again.

"Are you ready Ashrek? The sooner we are done the sooner you can get home to your wife and a hot meal."

"True, true! Not to mention her warm embrace." The men laughed together and walked back to the tunnel entrance. Ashrek tunneled further and then took a break, tunneled further again and took a break, Lord Vicrano following him deeper into the mountain.

"This should be the last part of the tunnel, about thirty mitras, I think." Ashrek was breathing heavily. "I think I need to take a break now. Perhaps complete it in the morning."

"Don't be ridiculous! We have come this far; I will not be stopped now. You are young and able. You will finish this tunnel tonight, now, Ashrek."

Ashrek looked Vicrano in the eye and could see the rabid determination there. He turned and looked at the men waiting behind them with support beams. With a sigh, he turned and faced the final wall of rock.

His arms trembled from the exertion, sweat dripped down his back. "Almost… there." He ground out through gritted teeth.

"LIGHT! I see light!" Lord Vicrano rushed forward. In his excitement, so eager to be the first through, he turned his back on Ashrek whose gaze had darkened with hatred.

A minor shift was all it took, "LOOK OUT!" Ashrek called, as a crack formed directly above Vicrano.

Lord Vicrano turned in time to see the look of hateful satisfaction on Ashrek's face before he was buried under the mountain he had hoped to conquer.

Ashrek looked around to make sure the workers had fled in fear before he used his gift to push down on the boulders covering Vicrano, to guarantee his death. He knew if enough blood remained in the corpse, Sybella would try to resurrect him. He took a certain amount of pleasure in squishing the man like the bug he was. He grasped a shard of rock and made a gouge down the side of his face and dropped a large boulder on his own hand, crushing it. He then emerged from the mountain covered in dust dragging the body, crying out in true agony.

"HELP! HELP US!" Men rushed to his side, lifting the broken body of Lord Vicrano. "I tried to warn him! He wouldn't listen." Ashrek sobbed, "he would not allow me to take a break. How will I tell Sybella?" Ashrek continued the charade until the wagon bearing him and the body of Lord Vicrano reached the manor. On hearing the commotion, Sybella and Lady Devona rushed outside.

"What happened? Where is my father?" Sybella glanced at the dust covered men and then her eyes landed on the cart. She walked silently forward and pulled the covering aside. Her eyes widened and then she leaned over the side and retched. He was completely unrecognizable; blood was smeared everywhere. She knew she would never be able to resurrect him. She turned to her husband who had a haunted look in his eye.

"WHAT happened?" Sybella shook with rage. Receiving no answer from her husband, she slapped him with all her might, whipping his head to the side and drawing blood.

From where Devona stood, she could see the rage flash across his face before the hysteria took its place. She slowed her hurried steps to watch the scene unfold.

"I tried to warn him! The men heard me time and time again tell him how dangerous it was. How unpredictable stone was, to stay behind me. But when we came to the final few mitras, I needed to rest. He would not let me. He rushed forward when he saw light ahead knowing the end of the tunnel was close. I cried out as I felt the mountain shift but he was too far away and I was too weak." Ashrek held his broken hand to his chest as blood dripped down into his eye. "I am so sorry my love. We will get through this tragedy together."

Sybella was visibly shaken as she led the way into the manor, her broken husband trailing behind her. As they passed, Devona moved to catch Ashrek's eye, she offered a slight bow and received only a scowl in return.

She wanted to laugh out loud! She would wait patiently for a moment when she could approach him and offer her assistance. Sybella would see just how comfortable the dungeon could be.

Chapter 38

ALRIC, ELAINEA, AKRONIUS AND NAIA had left the home of Shama with his blessing. The way down the mountain was much simpler than the journey up. Elainea had accepted the presence of Akronius as a necessary evil, but would not speak directly to him. Alric was the messenger and it was getting worse by the minute.

"Alric, can you ask Akronius when we can make camp? I'm tired and cold."

Before Alric could open his mouth, "Alric, please tell your sister we need to reach the base of the mountain to make camp; unless she plans to warm us all through the night with her charming personality?"

"Alric, please tell Akronius that I would gladly warm his cold unfeeling heart if he had one?"

"Alric, please tell…"

"ENOUGH! You two are worse than a pair of crows! Work it out or leave me out of it. Come on, Naia, let's go find something to eat."

Alric quickly walked away from them without a backwards glance. Naia took a moment to growl at them before bounding after him.

Nothing was said for a moment and then Akronius cleared his throat. "Listen, Elainea, I know you don't trust me. And you have every reason not to, but please believe me when I say I did everything I could for your mother. She was the best woman I have ever known and the closest thing to having a mother myself, no matter how short the time we had together. I would never, *could* never, harm her."

"This isn't about mother. Naia's account was enough for me to let go of that fear. This is about Alric and what happens next. He is all the family I have left and I will turn you into a bubbling puddle before I let any harm come to him. He may trust you, but I do not.

You changed once, what's to stop you from changing again? I will deal with you for his sake, and when the time comes for him to take the throne, you will leave us in peace."

Akronius could see the determination and fierce loyalty to her brother and for the first time, wished he had someone like that at his side. "You have my word." He extended his hand and she gripped it just as Alric walked back into the clearing with a large bird thrown over his shoulder.

"Praise The One! Finally, we can travel in peace. Elainea, please start a fire so we can roast this magnificent bird that Naia flushed out."

As they settled around the fire, Naia was the first to feel the tremors. She started whining and edged closer to Akronius. He looked around and then everyone was shouting in alarm.

"What's going on?"

"What is that?"

They felt the ground shaking and glanced back at the mountain where boulders were falling on the far side of the river.

"Can you see anything Alric?"

"It's too far away, but it looks like some men are trapped in a collapsed tunnel."

"There are no tunnels through the mountain Your Majesty. King David is building a road that will cross the river and travel around it to the docks of Vimeo, but there is no other direct route." Akronius said thoughtfully.

"I can only tell you what I see. Looks like one man is dead. The other is moving now, out of my range."

"King David discounts many things as random occurrences, it would be wise for you to keep this in the back of your mind. You never know what bits of information will be useful or can complete a puzzle in the future."

"Thank you Akronius. I will take your advice."

The four of them settled down for the night. They had a long way to go, especially since they would have to travel so far from the river to avoid the king's men who were creating the road.

♛

King David watched Sybella as she slapped Ashrek across the face. His stomach turned a bit when he saw what remained of Lord Vicrano. This was an interesting turn of events. He would have to see what Sybella's next move would be. She was a strong woman in her own right, but her people were a cutthroat sort and would never follow a woman no matter her prowess. Perhaps Ashrek would be the conduit through which she could rule, the man was foolishly led by his love for her.

For the time being, he would continue work on the trade road. If she could not rise to power, he would have little resistance in taking over, and once Chumbra completed his task, no one would be able to stop him.

Chumbra was busy making final preparations on the spell his master had asked for. He would have to travel quite far for the final item. He had it well hidden, but if anyone were to discover this most potent ingredient, he would lose his edge and possibly his life in the process. Chumbra approached the king's chambers and knocked.

"Come!"

"Pardon the intrusion Your Majesty, I will be leaving in the morning to gather the final ingredient. It will take approximately four days journey there and four days back. Within a fortnight, you will be the most powerful man living."

"Perfect, I will see you on your return."

The men parted ways and the king returned to looking in his spyglass. Sybella had taken the earrings off, so he was resigned to staring at the stone ceiling, but he could still hear her clearly as she spoke to a man, who he assumed to be either a soldier or an adviser.

"My father's death will not change our plans, you have my word. The road will be completed and when Ashrek is healed, he will finish the tunnel. The men are to hold their positions. I will send word for you when the moment is right to move. Stay alert."

"Yes, My Lady."

He could hear a door close and then open quickly again.

"Didn't I tell you I was not to be disturbed!" She sounded angry.

"But my love, you should not be alone at this time! Grieving as you are. Let me comfort you.”

"Do not touch me! This is all your fault! My father would be alive if not for your weak gifting! I regret ever marrying you! Leave me! I SAID LEAVE!”

"No. I don't think I will.”

The tone of his voice caused King David to sit up. Something was happening here.

"Ha! Finally growing a backbone are you, Dog? Too late! You will regret disobeying…”

King David heard a loud SLAP, followed by a thump.

"You would dare hit me! You know what I am capable of! Who I serve!”

She began chanting quickly. So dark was the spell she cast that the king could feel the malevolence through the connection. For a moment he heard nothing, then a wet gurgling before it was replaced with a deathly silence, broken with the gravelly voice of Ashrek.

"Do you think you are the only one with a strong gift, my love?” He spat the last word like it caused a foul taste in his mouth. "You surround yourselves with blood. You bathe in it. You drink it. You eat it. And yet you never stop to think of all the rich minerals contained in it. Minerals that I can control and bend to my will.”

David could hear scraping noises and gasps coming through the connection, how he wished he could see what was happening!

"Now, you will obey me in all things or I will bleed you dry just like your father. Am I clear? Good. Now sleep. You look terrible my dear. Grief does not become you.”

King David could hear a door gently close and then all was silent.

He jumped up, intending to summon Chumbra. Looking outside, he realized it was already dawn. The Oracle had probably left. He would have no choice but to wait for word on what had transpired in Vimeo.

Chapter 39

ASHREK LOOKED OVER AT HIS WIFE, her skin was ashen and her eyes dull. He was keeping her in a weakened state until he could blame her death on grief. By sapping the minerals from her body slowly, she looked as if she were wasting away. Despite what she ate or what spells she tried to perform; she just was not physically strong enough to compete with him. They had buried her father that morning and though she protested being seen in public, he had forced her; claiming her grief had so weakened her that she could not walk unsupported. Her people ate it up. Her eventual death would not come as a shock.

His father was scheduled to arrive in a few days' time and together they would assume power over Vimeo. Arcana would be fine under his uncle Alcherist, here they would have sole authority. The people of Vimeo were so abused and used to violence they would welcome a benevolent leader such as his father.

"Lord Ashrek, may I have a word?" she had waited several days to be sure of his position before approaching him.

"Lady Devona. How can I help you?" Ashrek knew who she was. He knew of her predilection for duplicity so he had an inkling of what she would offer.

"Maybe it is I, who can help you. You know of me I am sure and my... past indiscretions. I can assure you I am done with all that. My son, King David, sent me here hoping Sybella or Lord Vicrano would find cause for my death and he could be done with me. His ambition has no bounds. I only want to live out the remainder of my days peacefully."

"So, you say, but I have not heard an offer yet, Devona." She was no lady and he would not address her as such.

She felt the snub deeply, but would not let it show on her face. She was past her prime and they both knew it. The games being played now were too fast for her to keep up with. All she could do was bow out gracefully and hope to be set up in a way to live comfortably for all her efforts.

"My son has spies in the manor. He thinks I do not know of it, but I still have those loyal to me. He gave your wife a pair of spelled earrings. Through them he can hear and see what the wearer does. I am sure he knows of Lord Vicrano's death and already plots to gain control of Vimeo."

"Alright, I'll have them destroyed. Is that all you can offer me?"

Devona scrambled for more information. "He is seeking a spell that would give him the ability to absorb gifts. His Oracle, Chumbra, promised him such a spell existed and he is currently seeking the means to complete it. If you find Chumbra and kill him, you will cut off the king's ability to grow stronger. With your ability to move earth, you could overpower him easily."

Ashrek considered her words. If she told the truth, the information could help him gain his own kingdom and he wouldn't be under his father's thumb. Each of them would have their own people to govern while keeping power in their family line.

"I will look into this. For now, retire to your room until I call for you."

"Yes, my Lord."

"And Devona... don't go disappearing. Even invisible, the minerals in your blood will still call me." He smiled as he watched her face pale. He had his spies as well.

"You did WHAT?" Alcherist could not believe what he was hearing.

"Calm down brother! This is good news! You should be glad. Your wife was glad when she heard of Vicrano's messy end."

Lord Overton watched his nephew playing on the floor with several wooden toys strewn about. He was particularly fascinated with a horse shaped block.

"You went behind my back and had Ashrek kill him! You *knew* I wanted to avenge my family. That I *needed* to be the one to do it!

Are you even listening to me?"

Overton was distracted and slightly disturbed as the child put the toy in his mouth and proceeded to bite its head off. He spat it out and laughed eerily.

"Alcherist, is your son alright?"

"What...what do you mean?" He glanced over. "Children break toys all the time. Of course, he is fine. Do not try to change the subject Brother. You are wrong for this and I will not forget it."

Alcherist bent to pick up Khal and stormed from the room. Overton could have sworn the child's eyes went black, but when he blinked, they were the normal shade of green like his mother's.

He shook his head. He must be tired. Hopefully, Alcherist would not cause too much of a stir over his wounded pride.

Chapter 40

ALRIC AND AKRONIUS WERE TALKING SILENTLY as Elainea and Naia led the way. They both stopped when she cried out. Looking up, they realized the reason for her outburst. Their farm could be seen in the distance. They picked up the pace and were able to reach their home before nightfall. The siblings stopped at the door.

"I'll head to the river and do some fishing." Akronius said. He knew they would need some time. Coming back to an empty home would not be easy.

Alric was the first to step over the threshold. He inhaled deeply hoping to catch one last whiff of the woman who had raised him and loved him as her own. But too much time had passed. The siblings looked around the room that had held so many memories and let the tears fall. Finally, they placed their things down ready to face the final hurdle.

"Where is she?" Elainea asked Akronius who had returned with a pail of fish. Setting it down he quietly asked them to follow.

The four of them gathered around the mound of stones and wept silently.

"You picked the perfect spot." Alric said as they watched the sunset, "it's beautiful here. It's like she was watching us the whole time," he said staring into the distance at the mountain.

"That's because I was, dear ones."

All of them jumped up except for Naia, she was wise enough to know what was happening.

"Mother!"

"How can this be?"

"Mother!" Elainea wanted to run to her but Wleia held out her hand to stop her.

"All will be revealed in time, for now you must listen. Alric, a great evil is about to be unleashed on the entire land, not just

Elhaanai. You must be strong enough to face it, wise enough to accept help and discerning enough to recognize friend from foe. Elainea you must let go of the bitterness toward Akronius, he will be hugely instrumental in the days to come. Akronius you must trust your instincts and when you are presented with a gift more precious than you think you deserve… shut up and accept it, please. Now that your gift has been activated, you will meet your familiar, and no, it is not Naia. It will be a creature far more regal. Naia was a comfort to me and a help to you, but she must find her own path as well. Now my children, for you are all my children in one way or another; know that I love you, in my past life and in the one I live now. Move forward with my blessing and remember, Be strong and courageous!" She opened her arms wide as if to embrace them all, and each one felt her arms wrap tightly around them one last time before she faded away.

"Wow," Alric said.

"Yes, that was amazing." Elainea said, turning to Akronius, "I'm sorry. Mother is… was always right. We are good now. We are family."

"Are you going to cry Akronius? Are those tears in your eyes?" Alric ribbed Akronius.

"Of course not! It was the wind blowing your scent in my face!"

"Ha! He has you there, Brother."

"You're not so fresh yourself Princess!"

The three laughed as they headed back to the small house. The next day, Alric cornered Akronius.

"I have a request to make of you. Several actually."

"Anything, Your Majesty."

"Should anything happen to me, you will take care of my sister."

"That is asking a lot but you have my word." Akronius groaned at the thought.

"I want to see where my birth parents are buried."

Akronius paled and didn't answer immediately. He passed his hands over his face and sighed. "That will be difficult. Your father is entombed in the catacombs with other royals, so we can get there with some stealth but your mother, your birth mother... Devona had her cremated and used the ashes in several different spells.

"Wow, she really is evil huh?"

"You have no idea the lengths she is willing to go to obtain power. We must be very careful of her."

Elainea came out at that moment and glared their way. "I pity the man who falls for that fire sprite."

Alric laughed, "You're not the only one."

Chapter 41

AKRONIUS WANDERED OFF SHORTLY AFTER that to gather wood. As he was felling a tree, he heard a familiar sound. He whipped his head from left to right looking for its origin. Suddenly a shadow swooped down and landed on a nearby branch. He was in such awe that he could not speak.

"Have you nothing to say Akronius?" The bird said, cocking its head to the side.

"How do you know my name?"

"You kept me under lock and key for two years, how could I *not* know your name. You should be asking me for mine."

"You are right, my humblest apologies. What is your name, beautiful one?"

"I prefer handsome, thank you. My name is Auni. What are you doing out here?"

"Pleasure to make your acquaintance Auni. I am chopping wood for a fire. I am staying with friends, my family nearby."

"Friends or family?"

"Both. What are you doing out here?"

"I am afraid that during the time since my capture, my mate has abandoned me and taken another. She is not the one to blame." He stared pointedly at Akronius, "Consequently I am presently without a nest."

Akronius thought for a moment, positive that he must have gone mad. The bird was poisonous, but he seemed friendly, what if this was the regal muse Wleia had alluded to.

"Why are you not surprised that we can speak now when we could not before?'

Auni looked at him silently before answering. "It is common knowledge that we, Firauni, are often a familiar of those golden-gifted. While I was your captive, I could see glimmers of this golden thread from time to time. I knew it was up to The One whether he would accept you and awaken your true gift or not. When you released me, I knew for sure that you had altered paths. Though I am not your familiar, but I have tracked you ever since."

Akronius was both humbled and honored by this regal creature. "Would you like to come back with me, maybe the barn would be comfortable for you during the winter months. Temporarily, until you find a mate of course. And the door would remain open at all times of course, unless you got cold, then we could close it. If you wanted, but you would be free to leave at any time..."

"Akronius?"

"Yes?"

"Close your mouth! I will come with you. Everyone deserves a second chance. Even stupid men like you."

Wleia's words came back to him as if on the breeze and he smiled. He finished loading the wood into his cart and the two of them traveled back to the house.

"Took you long enough, Akronius, did you get lost?" Elainea asked.

"No, I ran into an old friend, sort of," he answered, glancing up and watching Auni glide down.

"Akronius, do you know what that is?" Elainea was positively bouncing with excitement, "it's a Firauni bird. Basically, the king of birds! They are almost extinct and are quite dangerous. How did you manage to befriend it?"

"It's a long story, but suffice to say, we are in a far better state now than when we initially met. Right, Auni?"

"I should say so."

Everyone else simply heard a chirp and took it for agreement.

"Elainea, did Alric tell you what he wants to do next?"

"Yes, he did. And I agree, it is something he should do. I only wonder if maybe it is something he needs to do alone. It is not my father after all."

"Alric, it is up to you. But the sooner we leave the better."

"Elainea, will you be alright here by yourself? A young woman alone..." a series of clicks, whistles and growls interrupted him.

Alric looked to Akronius for translation.

"They said she will be fine." He shrugged. He didn't need to go into detail of the threats made on anyone's life who would dare threaten their newly formed family. The two men prepared to leave at first light.

Before the sun had cleared the horizon, Alric and Akronius were on their way to the royal catacombs. It would take them several days to reach their destination and they would have to avoid towns at all cost. Akronius was sure the king had issued a warrant for his arrest and maybe even his life.

Chapter 42

KING DAVID PACED ACROSS THE DAIS of his throne room again and again. Akronius had betrayed him, he was certain of it. The man had essentially dropped out of existence. None of his trackers had been able to locate him and there had been no sign that he had followed Devona to Vimeo out of loyalty to her. He would have to bide his time and hope the man turned up eventually, and if he did, he would place his head on a spike and bleed him dry as an example of what happens to deserters. Out of the corner of his eye, he saw his spyglass begin to glow, meaning something was happening on the other end. He picked it up and came face to face with Lord Ashrek.

"Hello King David! I assume you are watching and listening. I'll get straight to the point; I am coming for you. I will have your throne, your crown and your life. You can thank your mother for providing this bit of information. Who knows what you might have witnessed had I never found out about this little spell. Would you like to thank her, your mother? She is right here."

Ashrek moved so that Devona was visible and what King David saw caused his breath to leave in a rush. His mother was propped in a bed looking terrified and unable to speak. Slowly she started to look like a corpse. Her cheeks began to sink in and her hair first lost its shine and then fell out in clumps. Her lips thinned and her frightened eyes clouded over with a white film. The bones on her hands stood out against paper thin skin. He could see her chest rise and fall so she still lived, but he knew it would not be for long. What had the man done to her? What kind of evil gift did he possess that he could drain her of life so quickly? Ashrek had not moved from the spot. He held the earrings. He had not touched Devona. Could it be a poison he had given her earlier? He had to find out.

"You see David. My wife Sybella, lies in much the same state. And you will soon join their ranks."

"And what do you think this knowledge will do to me? Am I supposed to cower in fear of you? Am I supposed to simply walk away from my throne? I do not know what magic you possess but you do not scare me. Soon there will be nothing that can harm me." He momentarily forgot that Ashrek could not see or hear him.

"And if you think your Oracle and the spell, he is preparing for you will be strong enough to save you, think again. It would be a shame if I caught up to him first wouldn't it? Would you be afraid then, David?" The smile on Ashrek's face actually caused King David to pause. Was it possible? Curse Devona and her willingness to trade secrets.

"I'll leave you to ponder that. Say goodbye to your mother, I have no more use for her." The last thing David saw was his mother's eyes widen in stark terror and then the heel of a boot crushed the earring causing his mirror to shatter in his hands.

"AAAARRRRGGGGHHHH!' King David flung the rest of the mirror into the wall in frustration. Even in death, she was still undermining his authority. He would have to be sure Chumbra made it back to the manor safely; only he had no idea where he had gone for the last ingredient. This was the one thing Chumbra had kept to himself, when pressed for the information, he would only say it was important that it remain a secret. King David had to hope that Ashrek was bluffing.

Akronius and Alric had made their way safely to the catacombs, and it was as Akronius had feared. They had passed several posters with his description listed for a reward; wanted dead or alive, and soldiers were everywhere. But, thanks to his heightened senses they were able to avoid detection.

"This is it Alric, I am not sure of the exact resting spot of your father but it should be further back in the tombs. The bodies closest to the entrance would be the oldest." Together they entered the tombs and made their way deep into the darkness. Because of the inky blackness, they were unable to tell how much time passed but it felt like hours. They needed no light. Alric held onto the back of

Akronius' shirt, and his wolfish eyes allowed him to see as if it were daylight. Still, by the time they reached the back of the crypt, they were both sweating and covered in grime.

"This is it. Your father's crypt is right here. This is strange." Akronius said, "the door is open." He drew his sword and crept inside with Alric just behind him.

"I may not make a habit of visiting crypts but shouldn't there be a body there?"

"Yes, there should, but it is not uncommon for dark Oracles to visit crypts hoping to harvest pieces of powerful men and women to increase the potency of their spells. I would not be surprised if..." He put up his hand for silence and cocked his head to the side just like Naia did. "We are not alone, hide!"

Akronius and Alric hid in an alcove just as a wall slid to the side and Chumbra stepped out. He glanced around the room carefully before lowering the face guard on a suit of armor, causing the wall to slide back into place. He scurried out and closed the crypt door behind him. Alric went to stand and Akronius held him in place a moment longer, his head still to the side and his eyes glowing amber. Finally, he released Alric and they stood.

"You know Akronius, your animal instincts are quite handy. I am glad you are on our side. I would hate to ever see you use that gift for evil."

"Thank you Prince Alric, I appreciate your words. Now let's see what sort of cheese our little rat hid in his hidey hole."

Chapter 43

ALRIC PUSHED THE FACE GUARD UP and the door slid open again, revealing a flight of stairs lit by some sort of glowing fungus.

"Don't touch it." Akronius sniffed, "It's poison."

"How do you know that? How are you doing any of this?"

"To be honest, I am not sure. Mother said to trust my instincts and I am trying to do that. It's like I can feel Naia in my head, and I call her to the front and use her senses to filter what I am facing. Sight, smell, hearing. It's all enhanced thanks to my bond with her. I will have to explore other animals to know the true extent of my abilities. But for now, this will do."

"Would it be wrong to say, I am a bit jealous. That would be a fun gift to have. Imagine how wonderful food must taste with all those senses!"

"You are always thinking of your stomach Prince Alric. Focus, what can you see?"

Alric looked on each side and then down the stairs. "We are below ground and there are several bodies below us. Only one seems to be moving. And very slowly, as if injured or perhaps chained."

"Good, let's go."

They reached the bottom and found themselves in a dungeon with several open cells. There was only one that was locked at the far end. The two men approached slowly only to hear…

"Back so soon Chumbra? And with company! You should have warned me so I could dress for the occasion. Come now, introduce our guest. Will they be sampling the wares as well? I hear there is a sale on blood these days. It's to *die* for." The voice chuckled slightly at his own joke, and Alric tried unsuccessfully to cover his own laughter. "Ahh, he has a sense of humor as well! Will wonders never cease."

"It can't be." Akronius stopped short of the open door.

"What is it?" Alric asked, "He is restrained. We should free him."

"WAIT!' Akronius shouted, but it was too late. Alric entered the cell without him.

"Hello there! Who are you? What did you do to end up chained here?" Alric bent to assess the chains binding the man. "Come now, don't tell me the prospect of freedom has dried up that well of humor. That was a pretty good one you told back there."

"Who... who are you, Boy?" the chained man asked quietly.

"Don't answer that." Akronius said from the shadows, "Do you trust me?"

"Yes, I do," Alric replied warily.

"Then I need you to step away from him for a moment. I need him to answer one question first, and then you can speak to him all you want."

Akronius entered the cell fully so the man could see him. His eyes widened.

"Do you recognize me, Sir?"

"I do," the chained man cursed through gritted teeth. "And if I were not chained, my hands would be wrapped around your traitorous neck. If Chumbra had not cast a spell on this place, I would have every insect within a mile eating your evil heart while it was still beating!"

Akronius nodded. "And it would be justified. It is for that reason that I will not release you until this young man introduces himself to you."

Akronius nodded again and stepped aside to lean on the wall. Alric looked between the two men with uncertainty.

"Okay then, how much exactly do you want me to tell him, Akronius?"

"Tell him only enough so that the information will identify him as friend or foe."

Alric considered this for a moment and then turned to the bearded man in chains. He was old and yet still muscular. He must have been someone formidable in his prime. The man's eyes widened as if he could hear his thoughts.

"I am Prince Alric Bear-Claw, son of Alanna and Kaison Bear-

Claw."

Alric placed his hand on his blade just in case the man turned violent, based on the information he had just provided. Instead the man covered his face and began to weep.

"Akronius, does crying fall under friend or foe?"

"Ha, ha, ha! She knew you would have my sense of humor!" The man said wiping his eyes, "and you have her silver eyes."

"What? You lost me…" Alric looked between the bedraggled man and Akronius.

"Your Majesty."

"Akronius, this isn't exactly the right time to show your allegiance to…." Alric realized that Akronius was not addressing him. He was bowing to the man in chains.

"It can't be…"

"Yes, it can, and it is. Alric, this man is King Kaison, your father."

The End

I really hope that you enjoy this story.

If you have a moment to leave me a review I would really appreciate it. Without reviews it is very hard to grow a book's audience.

With sincere thanks, Nicole

About The Author

THOUGH THIS IS MY FIRST full length novel, I have been writing poetry for as long as I can remember. I could be anywhere, doing anything when inspiration would strike. I have poems written on store receipts, brown paper bags, notebooks, anything that I had on hand became the recipient of my soul's love of the written word. I wrote for family and for church events. I wrote when I was happy and when I was heartbroken. Writing has always been the way I expressed my truest self.   Everyone in my family, and my church family, has been pushing me to write a book, but the timing was never right to me. THIS book flowed from my soul to the pages, I couldn't have stopped it even if I had wanted to.

In January 2020, my pastor delivered a message about being ready to move. I was ready to MOVE on so many different levels. I wanted to move professionally, physically, emotionally and spiritually. I went to the altar and offered everything to Him that day. My prayer was and still is, Lord, move me where you want me to be, please. That week God woke me up at 5am and gave me the beginning of this book. Word for word the first paragraph He told me. He gave me the name of the city. Each day I would pray, asking where the characters are going today. What are they experiencing? Feeling? I tried to force myself to write some days because I was enjoying it so much and often I would have to go back and delete or completely change what I had written. It couldn't be forced. I remember that first week every devotional I did was about creativity and listening for the voice of God. But of course I didn't do it alone, I got to a point where I didn't know what came next and my husband helped. He was amazing to bounce ideas off. The plot twist came from him and it was genius! This whole process has been God ordained and I am so, SO excited! Each time I re-read it, the excitement would return. I got to a point where I was happy and knew Book One was finished. (Yes, there will be more!). I am on a journey and really hope you will come along for the ride.

Follow along with me @NicolePatriceT on Twitter and IG.